Praise for Ardulum: First Don

A glorious love letter of a book, pushing the idea of what space opera can be and who it's written for, utilizing a complex web of science facts and science fiction concepts to ask questions about truth and history and who benefits.

\-   Seanan McGuire, author of *Every Heart a Doorway*

Award Finalist

Ardulum: First Don—Forewords INDIES finalist in science fiction

Ardulum: Second Don—Gold Crown Literary Society finalist in science fiction

The Ardulum Series:

Ardulum: First Don

Ardulum: Second Don

Ardulum: Third Don

Tales from Ardulum

Ardulum: The Battle for Pruitcu

Other books by J.S. Fields:

Foxfire in the Snow

Distant Gardens

Farther Reefs

Queen

Awry With Dandelions

Tales From Ardulum

Ardulum

J.S. Fields

Space Wizard Science Fantasy
Raleigh, NC
www.spacewizardsciencefantasy.com

Cover art by MoorBooks
Map by MoorBooks
Editing by Heather Tracy
Book Layout © 2015 BookDesignTemplates.com

Tales From Ardulum/J.S. Fields.— 2nd ed.
ISBN 978-1-960247-02-5

Author's website: www.jsfieldsbooks.com

For my daughter. May you one day steal a Buran and see the galaxy
you've long dreamed about.

CONTENTS

Mercy's Pledge ____ 7
Exile ____ 29
Just a Bar on Mars ____ 65
Palace Politics ____ 85
Youth Journey ____ 103
Subversion ____ 119
The Gift of Friendship ____ 135
Legacy ____ 155
Quality Time ____ 206
Glossary of Ardulan Talents ___________________________________ 215
Noteworthy members of the Charted Systems ___________________ 216
Noteworthy members of the Alliance ____________________________ 218

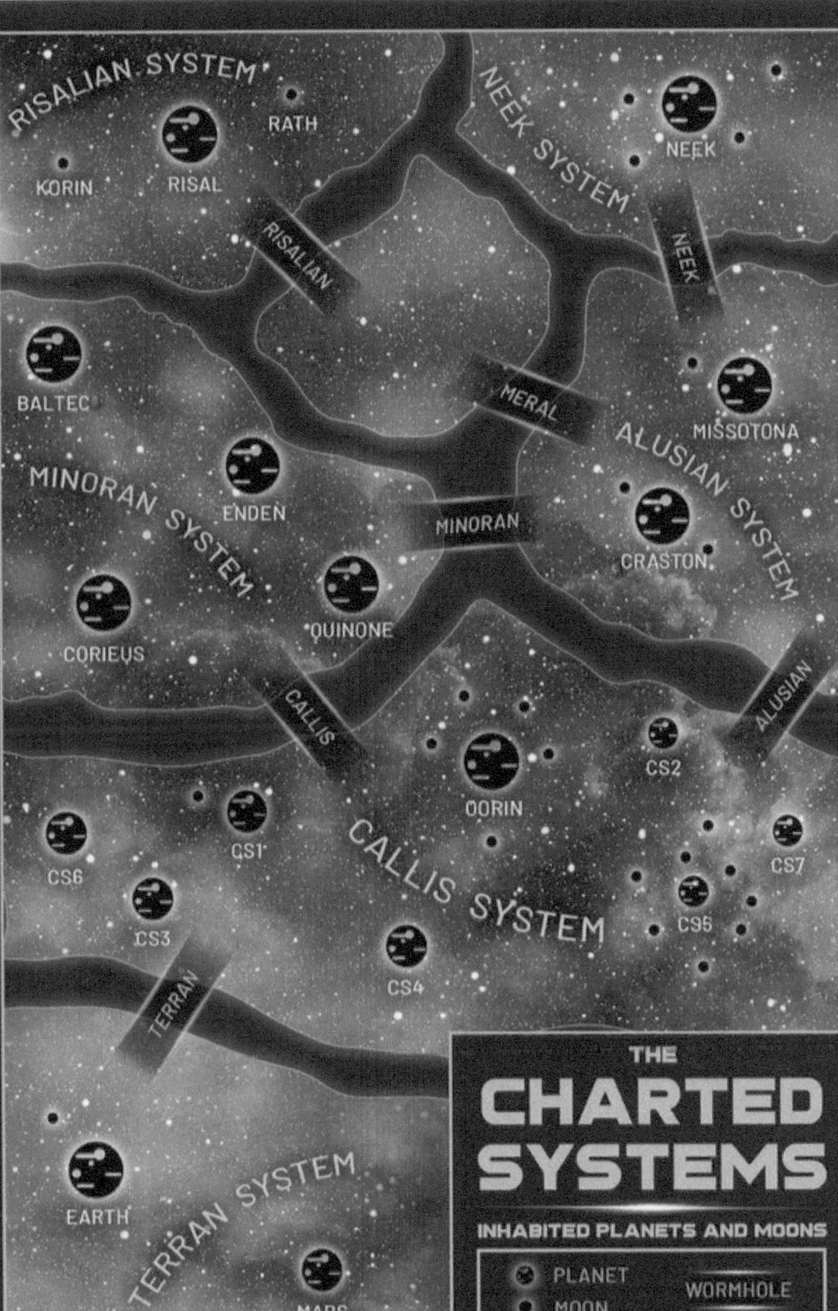
RISALIAN SYSTEM
RATH
KORIN
RISAL
RISALIAN
NEEK SYSTEM
NEEK
NEEK
BALTEC
MERAL
MISSOTONA
ALUSIAN SYSTEM
MINORAN SYSTEM
ENDEN
MINORAN
CRASTON
CORIEUS
QUINONE
CALLIS
OORIN
CS2
ALUSIAN
CS6
CS1
CS7
CS3
CALLIS SYSTEM
CS5
CS4
TERRAN
EARTH
TERRAN SYSTEM
MARS
THE
CHARTED
SYSTEMS
INHABITED PLANETS AND MOONS
PLANET
MOON
WORMHOLE
MAP CURRENT AS OF JAN 7, 2059 ACE

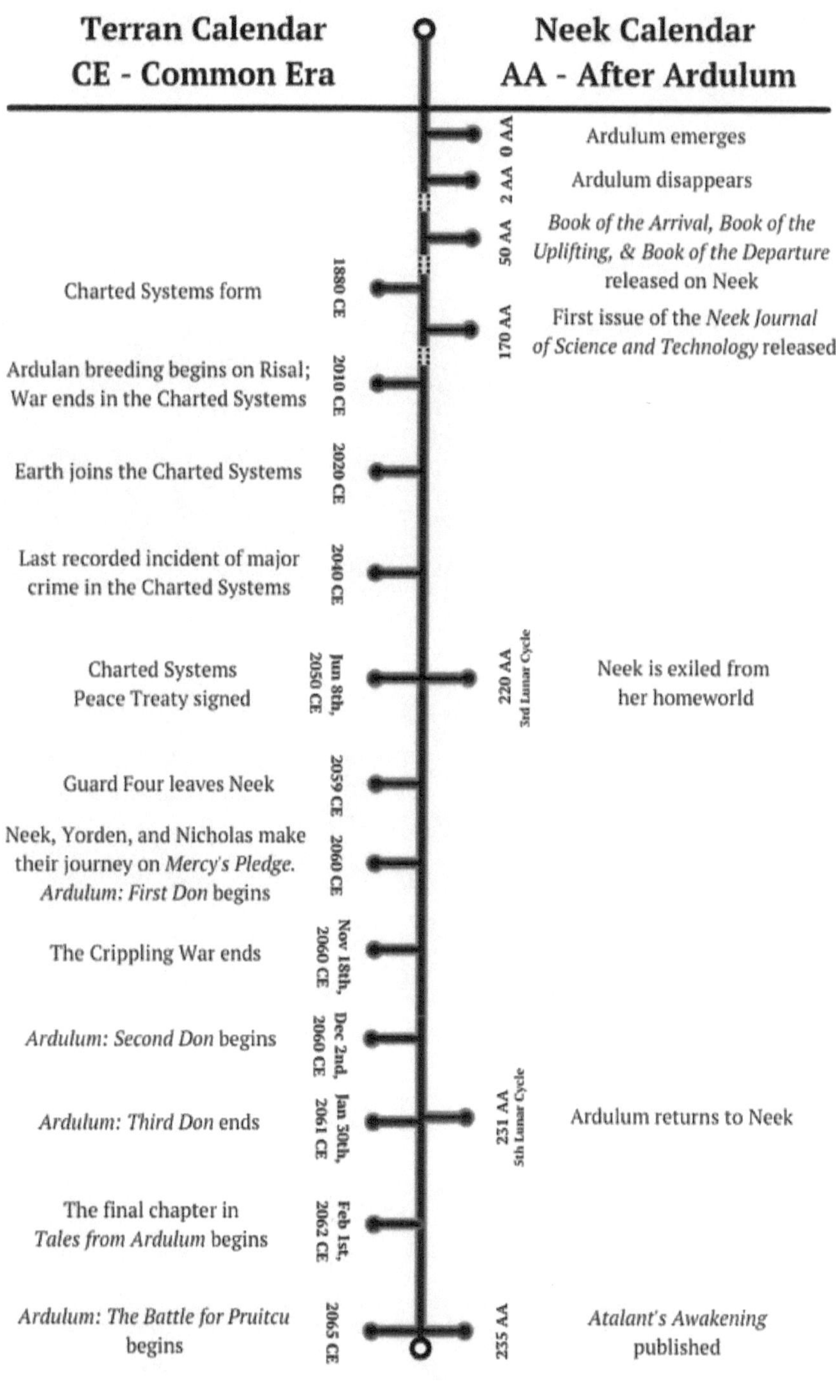
Terran Calendar
CE - Common Era
Neek Calendar
AA - After Ardulum
Ardulum emerges
0 AA
Ardulum disappears
2 AA
Book of the Arrival, Book of the Uplifting, & Book of the Departure released on Neek
50 AA
Charted Systems form
1880 CE
First issue of the Neek Journal of Science and Technology released
170 AA
Ardulan breeding begins on Risal; War ends in the Charted Systems
2010 CE
Earth joins the Charted Systems
2020 CE
Last recorded incident of major crime in the Charted Systems
2040 CE
Charted Systems Peace Treaty signed
Jun 8th, 2050 CE
220 AA
3rd Lunar Cycle
Neek is exiled from her homeworld
Guard Four leaves Neek
2059 CE
Neek, Yorden, and Nicholas make their journey on Mercy's Pledge. Ardulum: First Don begins
2060 CE
The Crippling War ends
Nov 18th, 2060 CE
Ardulum: Second Don begins
Dec 2nd, 2060 CE
Ardulum: Third Don ends
Jan 30th, 2061 CE
231 AA
5th Lunar Cycle
Ardulum returns to Neek
The final chapter in Tales from Ardulum begins
Feb 1st, 2062 CE
Ardulum: The Battle for Pruitcu begins
2065 CE
235 AA
Atalant's Awakening published

Mercy's Pledge

2030 CE

"Scrub it down. Start with the cockpit, then work your way back. No toilets on this thing, of course, because the astronauts used diapers way back when and most of these old models were just for animals, so that's a bright side." The museum curator—a short, thin woman with wavy, brown hair and pinkish skin—produced a half-hearted smile. She tapped a white panel on the starboard flank of the old decommissioned Soviet shuttle. Housed in the warehouse section of some museum in Kaluga, the ship was a Buran model, although it'd been modded so many times since its initial flight that Yorden Kuebrich doubted its insides looked anything like the historic photos.

"Yeah, I got it. No worries." Yorden ran his fingers through his beard in what he hoped was an endearing gesture rather than a creepy one, smoothed out the wrinkles on his too-tight coveralls, grabbed his cleaning kit, and walked up the shaky platform steps to the entrance of the shuttle. Cleaning the inside was going to take days, which was just fine. After the year he'd had in the Gaza Strip—not to mention the little heist he was planning—a bit of mindless cleaning while he worked out the details was exactly what he needed.

He grimaced at the rank smell of old oil and deteriorating plastic as he squeezed through the narrow walkways of the shuttle. Either the Soviets had been a *lot* smaller back then or Yorden had put on more weight in the past decade than he'd realized. Didn't matter. Muscle, fat, facial hair...it was all the same when you woke up every morning from nightmares of a friend killed, a family home destroyed, or a passive-aggressive act of one angry government against another. Who was right, who was wrong—it didn't matter then, and it didn't fucking matter now. The world was full of old decay. Religious cousins were still at each other's throats, although now they used words instead of bombs. And it was all stupid because there were *actual aliens*, turns out, flying around in space.

Aliens! Yorden snorted as he entered the tiny cockpit and set his cleaning kit down on a metal case. For ten years now, Earth had been part of the Charted Systems. For ten years, fucking aliens had been showing them how to use wormholes and cellulose tech and weird biometals, and here Yorden was, standing in a metal bucket containing a throttle-lever thing and analog controls after having fled yet another country he'd wanted to call home.

His first home, Poland, he'd left because fuck communism and fuck his early memories of the exorbitant price of meat and his family never getting a condo because the lottery was never in their favor. And fuck the lines. He was glad he'd never had kids, never needed to wait in line for twenty-four-plus hours just to buy a damn doll. Anyway, toilet paper was a goddamned miracle he never wanted to live without again.

Things got better in the nineties—but he'd been *done*. Naturally, Yorden had just managed to trade one tortured ideology for another. Israel. Gaza. He was Jewish, in that ham-eating, post-Soviet way. Still, birthright. Homecoming, sort of. It was enough to pull him in. Enough to convince him to try out settling there. That had failed miserably. It was just a different kind of death out there: a faster one, from bullets and bombs.

That was all over now, though, because of Charted-fucking-Systems-mandated *peace,* but nothing could erase his memories. Thus, Yorden was back in Eastern Europe, on a dilapidated shuttle, preparing to install the Cell-Tal components hidden under his cleaning kit and in his bag, so he could fly this hunk of metal off Earth and get into the Systems proper. Yorden grinned. Off Earth, out of this solar system, and away from the crush of history. Away from *his* history. Away from the politics and the false smiles and the lovey-dovey crap everyone spewed now instead of the thinly veiled racist ideology of the past. People didn't change—Yorden didn't believe they could, not for a hot minute. *Humans* sure as hell didn't change. Aliens might have brought technology based on turning trees into spacefaring biometals, and they might have brought peace, but neither of those came without a price. If he was going to live a lie, then better if he did it on his terms, in space, where it was a hell of a lot easier to avoid everyone.

So, forget Earth. Forget Mars, even. He'd take "diaspora" to a whole new level.

"You doing okay, then?" The curator's voice reverberated within the metal, making Yorden wince. "Some of that stuff up in there is pretty delicate."

"Yeah, I got it! I'll do the gun turret last since it's not part of the original structure and looks like it wasn't put on well to begin with. I don't know what you guys thought you'd need to shoot with this, other than the peace-toting Risalians that came knocking at our solar door ten years ago." He paused and considered the walls and his very heavy gear bag stuffed with Cell-Tal tech. "I'm going to have to take the wall panels off, too, to clean. I think you've got mice."

An expletive came from the curator, although Yorden wasn't certain what language it was in. Not Russian or Polish—he was sure of that. Definitely not Yiddish. Since she was already upset but clearly not willing to come in and inspect the "damage," Yorden added, "Probably best to strip her down to the floor and walls anywhere I can. If you've got one nest, you've got ten, and I don't think you want to pay a guy to redo wiring, right?"

"Do what you can and just...make it look right on the outside, okay? No one is ever going to look under the panels. It's not like this Buran is ever going to fly again. That laser was never even fired, from what I know. It was attached quickly. Apparently, humans didn't want to give up their guns when the peace treaty was signed. Not that it does any good on a ship that can't fly."

"Oh, she'll fly," Yorden muttered. He waited until he heard the door to the hangar slam shut, followed by the screeching of the wide bay doors to the warehouse closing, and then peeled a clump of old metal and coated wires from the wall. He would put it all back together again, snug as a bug. He just needed to make a few modifications of his own first.

* * *

"You've got a week left. Sure you'll make it?"

Yorden pretended to look offended.

The Alusian on the other end of the comm—a biped with purple, furred arms and legs and a smattering of teal scales across the rest of her visible skin—made a sound very much like a Terran clearing their throat. "I apologize for offending, but we do have a contract."

"I said I'd do it, so I'll do it. Calm down, Captain Neigh."

The purple arm fur rippled with irritation. "My name is Neganondonu," she said, curling the U sound up like at the end of a question. "Not 'Neigh,' not 'Donahue,' and not 'Meg,' all of which you've used at some point in the last three days. If the Charted Systems is your goal, then your pronunciation range is going to have to get a lot wider. I need those cedar trees on time, and I need the Risalians to not know about it. Can you or can you not deliver?"

Yorden took a deep breath, staring at the little computer monitors in the cockpit, just about the size of his palm, that were the last parts he needed to remove before installing his own Cell-Tal versions. He could do a week. He only had, what, two days of real work left? And then it was just the mechanics of getting an ancient shuttle out of a museum and into space. He had the chipped trees already. Brought the packets in during broad daylight on a forklift. The curator had asked about five questions before Yorden had flashed her his art restorer's license. As far as she knew, the wood was for repairs. After all, no one on Earth had any idea yet how cellulose tech really worked. He could have nailed a branch to the wall and called it a biometal for all that most people understood the mechanics. Still, he'd then asked if she wanted to file a complaint with the Risalian sheriffs. She'd backed down. Yorden didn't blame her. Filing a complaint would result in more paperwork than an injury claim through OSHA, and violent crimes were so rare now that if he *was* doing something, it was unlikely to be something horrible.

Yorden wiped his nose on his sleeve. Crime. It'd always been fascinating what various governmental bodies thought was okay to do or what would get you arrested. The Risalians had simplified everything, and Earth's population had definitely calmed down...somehow, but getting Spanish cedar cut from the Amazon rainforest was still surprisingly easy to do, even with all the protections in place. The Risalians might have wiped out major crime, but they hadn't wiped out poverty. The "illegal" gold mining in the region—the Risalians weren't policing environmental destruction, after all—would have the banks of the Madre De Dios river eroded so far in another decade that the trees would be underwater, anyway. At least now, the trees would be of some use. He could pretend that the ethics of illegal logging bothered him, but memories of gunfire and going hungry still made his hands shake. The trees could figure out how to take care of themselves.

"I've got five eight-meter-diameter trees, flaked as requested, shoved into the newly remodeled cargo hold. The biofilms you lifted from Cell-Tal's warehouse integrated just fine into the analog circuitry, and the computer upgrades are happening today. It will be done on time."

"And the Risalians?"

Yorden flicked his hand in a careless motion, although his stomach did a little flip. "What interest could an ancient Terran shuttle possibly be to the sheriffs of the Charted Systems? This piece of junk doesn't even look drivable from the outside, much less flyable. Any scans they do of the cargo will just pull up wood. Hauling cedar isn't illegal, not even in Peru."

Captain Neganondonu's fur kept rippling, so Yorden sucked in a bellyful of air and tried again. "Look, if I get searched...I don't know. I'm just an upstart Terran looking to make a quick diamond in the black-market scents trade. I wouldn't be the first to try to sell Terran cedar as a biological weapon. I'm not cutting into any andal profits—no one in their right mind would touch that fucking tree since the Risalians buy every board of it they can find. It doesn't even grow on this world—can't, apparently. Needs some micronutrient our soils don't have. So, there's nothing to link me to you, unless you have some ties to whomever lifted the Cell-Tal parts."

"The parts went through four couriers. They're as clean as they can get. You are the only question mark in this operation."

Yorden forced out a tense smile. He'd smuggled before, of course, but never anything of this value, and definitely never off-world. Risalians were an unknown quantity, but it was easy enough to pretend they were harmless, even if he did dream about being behind bars, guarded by blue-skinned aliens. Hell, he had a lot of bad dreams these days. Risalians were the least of his worries.

"I've got this. Don't worry. See you in three days, tops. Kuebrich out." He turned off the little, round pocket comm and slid it into his coveralls. "Computers, computers," he muttered. "Two days to get these damn things in."

He slapped open his metal toolbox and lifted the top section out. Below were twenty or so sheets of thin biofilm crisscrossed with circuitry Yorden couldn't even begin to understand, but that didn't mean he didn't know how to install them. He'd been weaned on computers, after all, in the late eighties and early nineties. Cellulose tech was barely in its infancy when the Risalians came around, of course, but Yorden was clever. He'd studied engineering in Poland. His father had been a carpenter. Computer chips were just tiny carvings, and cellulose was just a filament to be wound, same as any wire or plastic. That andal cellulose always felt warm and made the hair on his arms stand on end was irrelevant.

Yorden studied the cockpit, which was so tiny that he could touch the left and right walls simultaneously. It'd never been meant for human transport, but with the advancement in spacefaring tech in the past twenty years, most of the components inside the cockpit were no longer necessary. He'd already removed the interior side panels, the base metal structure that kept anyone from moving about freely, and most of the center console. He'd replaced the main throttle lever with a yoke—a black one from some old video gaming system, but it fit and had the right parts—and the upper panels were now pressure-sensitive biofilms. Once he replaced the three small computers' innards with the stuff in the toolkit and got a power source, he could hook the whole thing together and, in theory, the Buran would fly. If he could manage to shove a few chairs into the cramped cockpit, it'd be a small miracle, but he'd stand all the way to the Terran Wormhole, and beyond, if it got him off this damn planet.

Yorden got down on his knees, crammed his hip and shoulder uncomfortably against the starboard wall, and tugged the first archaic monitor from its housing. The metal flaked around his hand, and when he went to flick the pieces off, the glass screen shattered.

Yorden's stomach sank. He snarled and ground his teeth as memories crashed around him. Of his friends dying. Of being hungry. Of wanting to be in control of his destiny for one damn minute.

"Fuck me."

Now what? It still had to mostly look like the original, or if the curator did a spot check, she'd flip her shit. Yorden tried for the lower central monitor—much more cautiously—but the same thing happened. Moreover, the left monitor, upon closer inspection, appeared to have suffered from repeated impact at some point. Breathing sideways on it could have sent the thing apart. Fantastic. That left Yorden standing amongst metal curls and broken glass, as well as the little end snips of Cell-Tal bioplastic sheets he'd had to cut to size for the interior of the computer banks. And no one wore shoes anymore because it wasn't fashionable in the Charted Systems—Yorden couldn't get a job if he *did* wear shoes—which meant he was going to end up with some nasty lacerations and a bunch of questions as to how they got there. Art restorers were not, as a general rule, supposed to break everything they touched.

Yorden pulled an old tablet from his pocket and scrolled through the online options. His thumb slicked over the cellulose weave as his hand shook. Damn it, he was better than this. He could handle a minor setback. There was no reason to get so upset. It wasn't like there weren't other ways to get off Earth. This was just the one with the fewest strings.

So, how to deal with his monitor problem, which was directly related to his power problem since he couldn't access the second without the first? He could have a replica made and delivered in two weeks. He could wander around a ship scrapyard and hope to get lucky, but the nearest yard wasn't open on Sundays because the owner was, ironically, from the USA.

Yorden sighed. He'd had enough of Earth for a lifetime. Hell, even Mars would be better than this planet filled with false peace and broken promises. Something was *wrong* here, and the bandage the Risalians had patched over it wasn't any better. It was worse, in a way, because Yorden at least understood war and religion and communism and all the other stuff humanity cooked up to kill one another. Whatever was going on right now was...it stank like gefilte fish, and Yorden fucking hated fish.

So, what then? His only real option was to do an open remod' and hope the curator never stopped by. There was probably something toxic in the dust and shards at his feet, so maybe he could keep her out that way. Really, it was a miracle the ceiling hadn't fallen in on him yet.

"Galactic criminal today, or galactic criminal tomorrow? Does it matter? Probably not." Delaying the departure date would be a hassle, but less of a hassle than trying to cover up his mistake or having to listen to a lecture by the museum curator who would *want* to be mad and throw things and have him arrested but wouldn't because of Risalian peace.

Fucking peace.

Yorden snorted and pulled apart the remains of the center console, keeping the section with the yoke intact. He laid the series of computer biofilms across the skeletal remains of the framework and then began to install the cellulose battery pack. It would independently power the navigation systems and computer itself, but not the thrusters, leaving only the question of how to get the hunk of metal off Earth. Yorden had one more deal to make before he could accomplish that goal.

* * *

Yorden primly folded his hands across his lap as he wedged his hips into the black leather chair he'd installed in the Buran's cockpit—a chair that had, until very recently, been in the curator's office.

"Yes, I am very interested in the safety of our youth. To me, Youth Journey—this time of directed internship and socialization, if you will, of the Systems' young people—has only the noblest of intentions. That's why I want to be a part of it, you see. Earth didn't join the Charted Systems until 2020, and I was thirty-five then. Far too old to take part in yet another birthright tour, but I think this ship and I have a lot to offer the youth of today." Yorden reached over and smacked the metal wall of the shuttle, which was in full view now that the Buran's new transmitter was up.

The Risalian on the other end of the comm stared impassively. Hir black hair was piled in a bun atop hir head, hir skin was the same sort of blue Yorden had seen in the history vids, and hir neck slits—gills, maybe—gently flapped open and closed like a gasping fish's mouth. The image wasn't disturbing at all.

"History!" Yorden added, continuing his charade, this time with more bluster. "Why, in this ship alone, I can tell the history of the Terran people! Our glorious journey into the stars! Or, rather, the Risalian discovery of our solar system and how everyone on Mars Colony practically wet themselves when your delightful blue faces showed up on the surface."

"Mr. Kuebrich, your allusions to Terran bodily functions can be left out of your application."

"Sure, sure. What do you say? You've got a pack of old thruster power modules over in Chiang Rai that'll work just fine for this shuttle, and I can have them here *tomorrow* with your okay. Give me a few days to get my bearings, and then I'll head to Callis Spaceport with a smile under my beard and a cockpit seat for a fresh young face."

"You haven't even sent me the safety specs of this shuttle." The sound of bioplastic films sliding against each other filtered through the comm. "What is your ship's name? *The Buran*?"

"No, no. It's...the *Pledge. Mercy's Pledge*, because, uh, I pledge to help kids find their way in life. It's my mission statement." Yorden was in danger of vomiting after saying that, but since the Risalian's neck slits hadn't even begun to shade into purple, it looked like he was on solid footing.

The Risalian straightened hir pale-yellow tunic and read something offscreen. Yorden had never seen a Risalian in person, only over comm, and found himself wondering if the species wore pants. Hell, he didn't even know if they had external genitalia. There was probably a first-contact video from Mars he could look up if he really wanted to, which, Yorden decided, he did not.

"Mr. Kuebrich, your résumé seems to have some contradictions. You note five Terran years of ship maintenance and three of piloting, but twelve of 'intergalactic diplomacy.' I see no degree certificate for this. Where did you study?"

"School of Hard Knocks," Yorden shot back, regretting the words the moment they left his mouth.

"Which is where?" xe asked.

"America. Texas. One of those smaller public schools no one ever talks about but that turns out decent people."

"I don't have enough records about the educational systems on your world to validate that answer." Xe rubbed at hir neck slits—not a good sign—and then clacked hir claws together. "I'm curious enough, given our lack of Terran mentors, to interview you in person. We've no use for those fuel cells anyway. They're too outdated. I'll have them shipped to you immediately. I can take your location from your comm signal. In three days, please be at the coordinates I am transmitting now."

"Perfect!" Yorden couldn't contain his grin. The curator had wanted some sort of fuel or thruster set for the shuttle, just to be able to show kids how one might hook them up. He'd get the Risalian tech installed no problem, and if she got upset about the different planetary origins...well, she'd likely just give him a lecture. Besides, once everyone figured out what he'd done, he'd already be in space, away from his miserable blue marble of a homeworld, and in a ship that might not fall apart for a few years. He'd have diamond rounds in his pocket from the cedar delivery and a whole new life to live. As long as the Charted Systems had some form of edible red meat that wasn't still walking around, he'd be happy.

* * *

Spaceship stealing turned out to be really easy.

Yorden had opened the bay doors and no one had even come by to ask why. He'd started the clean-energy thrusters, which had some fancier Risalian name that he didn't care about, and the curator had finally come by to ask if systems testing was important for museum pieces. Yorden had assured her that it was, and she'd left. And when he'd driven the marshmallow-shaped ship out of the museum and into the parking lot filled with the midday tourist crowd, the patrons had just cheered and taken photos with their phones. So, Yorden had pointed the *Pledge*'s nose to the sky and engaged the thrusters. Boom. Done. He hadn't even charred anyone standing too close because thrusters didn't put out that kind of heat anymore. Nope. He'd just sailed like a turkey vulture into the heavens while the sheep of his homeworld watched and thought it was the best damn thing they'd ever seen.

And now, he was here. In space. On a space station called Callis Spaceport and *fuck*—he was in space flying a ship he should have named *Stay Puft*. And he was talking to aliens.

"Two hundred and twelve diamond rounds, as agreed. Please release the locks on your hold and my people will unload the wood." Captain Neganondonu, arm fur rippling in what Yorden hoped was happiness, placed her palm on his old, rigid tablet to sign for the transfer of funds.

They were just outside the *Pledge*, which was cooling off in berth 3,504, docking bay nine, in the aft hangar of Callis Spaceport. Around them—stacked on either side, below, above, and diagonally—were thousands of ships. The *Pledge* was by far the smallest, dwarfed by frigates, liners, cutters, dredgers, and shuttles that made his look like a kid's paper airplane. The recycled air in the hangar smelled like burnt wood and salt, and the temperature was set several degrees too high for his liking.

"This...was not my brightest idea," Yorden murmured as his gaze wandered around the bay, his fingers twitching in his pockets. He knew that his eyes were as wide as saucers but didn't really know how to help that. Vertigo hit him in every direction, even when he looked to the side. The hangar was just... It was just huge. It was huge, and he was a Terran without a clue on a stolen spaceship left over from the Cold War. Hell, save for his pocket comm, the highest bit of technology he had was a tablet from 2015.

Why had he thought this was a good idea?

Words streamed from Yorden's mouth, bypassing his brain entirely. "No wonder Terrans don't generally go past Jupiter's diamond mines. There have to be millions just in this spaceport alone, and how can they all just live here in peace? What if I...what if I step on someone? Or sneeze and kill someone with my germs?"

Captain Neganondonu jiggled the tablet. "Calm down. While you walk and gawk, maybe the first thing you should buy is a new one of these. The cellulose content in your tablet here is so low that the metal feels cold, and I don't see anything resembling a biofilm. Cell-Tal ships to Earth, and I know they contracted with this fruit company."

Yorden shoved the tablet into the pocket of his snug flightsuit, ran a hand through his beard, and pursed his lips. He definitely wasn't shaking, and he definitely didn't feel like a LEGO mini figurine in an oversized toy box. "Yeah, I'll think about it. Meantime, can your crew spray down the inside of my cargo hold after you get the wood out? That smell gives me a headache."

"Of course, Captain."

A shiver ran down Yorden's spine. *Captain.* It sounded too good to be true. It sounded like how the air smelled in the Callis Spaceport—like a new paperback you stuck your nose into and huffed. Maybe someday he'd feel silly for getting so excited over a title conferred on him by a stolen ship. Right now, though, it sounded better than a hot shower or a trip to the barber or one of those really satisfying dumps you took after eating spicy food.

"How long till you finish unloading?" Yorden asked. His voice *definitely* did not sound nervous.

"An hour local time. Have you synced your watch yet? Callis runs on Systems Standard Time. Twenty-nine-hour days, which I think is a bit long for you."

Yorden tapped the bioplastic bracelet on his right wrist. It showed 12:03/29. "Auto-sync. I'm good. I'll just head for a walk. Be back at thirteen."

The fur on Captain Neganondonu's arm flattened as she turned from Yorden and continued to direct her crew. Yorden filled his lungs with that rich, too-good-to-be-true spaceport air and followed the blinking neon signs and flashing floor lights to the bay exit. The signs were either embedded in the walls, floating, or simply suspended from the ceiling, and they sported at least half a dozen languages. "Common" ran from right to left at the bottom of each—as mandated by Risalian law, but Yorden didn't think the made-up language was ever going to take off. Beings got particular about their heritage and such, or at least they did on Earth. Likely, Common would go the way of Esperanto. Still, he'd learned to speak it anyway, because he sure as hell couldn't pronounce Risalian sounds, and his Alusian was barely passable. A few of the signs had Spanish and Mandarin on them since Earth and Mars hadn't managed to agree on one representative language for the Systems, but the grammar was wrong on both and the spelling atrocious.

Some ten minutes later, Yorden finally wound his way out of the docking bay and into a brightly lit hall. Yorden let out a sigh of relief. The ceilings here were lower and the walls closer together. There were more signs—hundreds of them flashing and playing music and talking at him—and there were people. Beings. Sentients. Whatever they were called. Distinct bouquets of pheromones and body odors slapped his nose. No one seemed to be in much of a hurry, not this far from a central artery, but there were still just so *many* of them. Bipeds. Quadrupeds. Slicks of goo with voice-box things. Fur, feathers, scales, gasses, all chatting and eating and laughing. And there were Risalians in the corners, in the alcoves, and in the junctions, just watching with their stony faces, sometimes standing next to emaciated bipeds with translucent skin who seemed just as impassive.

Yorden pushed past them all, ignoring the occasional call to chat or drink or question if he was lost. His stomach was doing little flips, which were at least more manageable than the nausea-flips he'd had in the docking bay. A stiff drink would have settled it all, but he was already late thanks to the *Pledge*'s cheap navigation core. He'd need to upgrade that soon. Hell, he'd need to upgrade the whole damn ship soon.

"Yorden Kuebrich, please, over here."

Yorden turned in the direction of the heavily accented Common. His eyes widened. He'd expected the Youth Journey official who'd helped supply him with the thrusters or at least another yellow-clad Risalian. He wouldn't have been surprised if one in gray had shown up, either—some secretary or peon sent to deal with the Terran. But no, it was a blue-tunic that gestured for him to follow into an office off the main corridor. He followed hir into a room with a shimmering silver floor, smelly aquariums for walls, and a bay window that looked out onto a clear section of space. The whole place screamed money and power, and it was definitely not where Yorden wanted to be.

"Have a seat, Captain."

Yorden sat down on a thick chair, the seat made of a near ebony-colored wood he assumed to be andal. This was a Risalian, after all, and Cell-Tal was built on Neek andal plantation farming. In an office like this, no cheaper wood would do.

"Markin?" he asked. "'Cause the blue tunic—"

"Markin Kelm." Xe sat down on hir own wooden chair behind a narrow andal desk. The whole setup looked comically Terran. Yorden suppressed a laugh. "You are piloting a stolen historic ship and have a hold filled with timber you did not pay for."

Everything in Yorden froze save for his heartbeat, which only pounded louder. A swishing filled his ears. Were the Risalians always so blunt, or was this a tactic? Was a blaster going to come out from behind that polished desk and shatter the whole illusion of peace? God, Yorden really hoped so, even just so he could say, I told you so.

"Yeah," he managed. "So what?"

Markin Kelm gave away no emotion. "You understand that is illegal. All of it."

"Yup."

There was a long pause, then, as the markin stared at Yorden and Yorden stared defiantly back. The worst the markin could do would be to incarcerate him. They didn't kill beings in the Charted Systems. He'd heard of reeducation centers, but only in relation to the Risalians themselves, as they'd kept their own penal code for their people. If Kelm was trying to intimidate him, xe would have to work a lot harder than a guaranteed bed with three perf squares a day on some moon.

"Do you plan to continue such activities outside your solar system?"

Yorden shrugged. He looked cool, surely. Nonchalant. His brown hair probably needed a combing, and he definitely needed a shave, but that all, hopefully, added to his rugged charm. As long as Risalians didn't have heat sense to see that he was sweating like a roasting goat, he'd be fine. "Probably. Why? The museum trying to get its ship back?"

Kelm rubbed hir neck slits. "I have already compensated the museum for its loss, and a crew of workers is currently in the Amazon rainforest, replanting the species of tree you cut down."

Yorden raised an eyebrow. "That's got to be sticky work."

"For a Risalian or a Terran, perhaps. We have genetically unrelated workers who will not mind."

"Uh-huh. So, you've cleaned up my mess. What does that mean? I owe you?" Yorden scoffed. "Since I didn't care about the mess, you'll have a hard time collecting."

"I'd like to offer you a job, Captain."

That shut Yorden up. He leaned against the back of his chair, folded his arms across his chest, and considered the being in front of him. He'd read this spy book, surely. Some cheap, grocery store checkout lane plot where the hacker gets hired by the government or they go to jail.

Yorden snorted. He'd pass. He wasn't about to trade one shitty life for another.

"Like work release? Keep me busy instead of incarcerate me?"

A low growl came from the markin's throat. The copious hair on Yorden's arms rose for a moment until he realized that Kelm was doing the equivalent of a sigh.

"Captain, you have a very...unassuming ship with old technology. Your weaponry is laughable, but your hold has exactly the format of climate control required for live-tree shipment. I'd like to hire you for andal transport from the Neek homeworld to Rath, one of our moons."

"Where the Cell-Tal headquarters are?" Yorden couldn't keep the surprise from his voice. "One of your cutters could haul fifty times what the *Pledge* can carry." *What's the catch? There's always a catch. Probably has Risalian versions of AK-47s hidden in the trunks of those andal trees.*

Markin Kelm's left front claw clicked on the tabletop. That particular claw was longer than the rest, although Yorden didn't know if that was cosmetic or evolutionary. He'd thought Risalian claws were generally black, too, but Markin Kelm's longest was a pale green. It was juvenile to think of it as a giant booger picker, but the thought was already there, pushing laughter up Yorden's throat when there should have only been seriousness. He barely kept himself in check.

"When we are seeking to carry harvested plantation trees from the Neek System, I agree with you. However, transporting live trees is...something of a religious problem for the Neek. They are inherently wary of technology and find our cutters disconcerting. Yours, on the other hand, would pose little threat."

"Gee, thanks."

"In return, all charges against you will be dropped. You will be paid per transport, and the contract will continue as long as *Mercy's Pledge* is in operation." Kelm unrolled a thin tablet and pushed it across the desk to Yorden. "Sign where indicated and you are free to go."

Yorden didn't even bother looking at the biofilm. The contract stank worse than Yorden did. He was a Terran, sure, but he wasn't uneducated or some freshly minted Journey youth. The Risalians could take their sketchy-as-hell tree-shipment business and find some other asshole to run it. Unless the Risalian was willing to offer a lot more. Like a Minoran luxury liner. Or his own moon. Or hell, a house on a moon with a few scantily clad, fully consenting women and enough money that he never had to see another human again. Aside from his scantily clad ones, of course.

"You can't afford what I want."

The Risalian's claws clacked against the table. "We pay very well. We might only ask for three or four runs in a given cycle. You'd be free to take other jobs in the interim or simply relax."

"I'm not interested." He'd meant to stand in a huff—maybe kick his chair and storm out—when he caught sight of a sickly bipedal form in a shadowed corner. Yorden could only see half of a face and a shoulder, but the skin was a sunken, translucent copper. Revulsion rose in his throat before everything got still. Really still. His fingers pulled back from the edge of the chair arms. He folded his hands in his lap. His face relaxed, and the wrinkles on his forehead smoothed. There was still anger there—Yorden could feel it somewhere in his head—but it seemed too far in to bother with.

"The contract?" Markin Kelm prodded.

"Hey, I *want...*" Yorden trailed off. A thought bubbled up from...he didn't know where, but it wasn't from his brain and *that* was more worrisome than the blue iguana sitting in front of him. Information. He wanted information on how the Charted Systems worked and how the governing bodies worked and who—*what*—was responsible for the invasive peace. That information, his not-brain said, was worth more than his own moon or dancing girls and would be the key to him surviving in the Systems.

Information wasn't bad, Yorden argued with himself. In certain circumstances, it was worth more than diamond rounds. Still, he was being led and toyed with, and he didn't like it. His brain felt slimy, like he'd sucked in a snot ball too far. He checked his mood before answering. He couldn't manage to summon anger—not the kind he wanted—but disgruntlement was still available. He might also be able to manage indignation.

"I want to chat. How did you Risalians manage all this?" Yorden pointed to the door. "All of this peace and love and getting along? Tell me why my urge to strangle you seems to have fled."

"That isn't relevant to our conversation."

"No? Okay, well, how about this one: Where did the Terran Wormhole come from? Our scientists knew nothing about it until one of your cutters popped out and scared the shit out of everyone."

"The wormhole was always there. Your people just didn't know how to activate it."

"Bullshit. Why are you so damn *polite*? We're in here like we're having tea, not like I stole a *priceless piece of history*, stripped it of its historic value, raped one of the few remaining old-growth forests on Earth, and sold it on the Systems' black market. Why am I not in detention right now? Why are you letting that Alusian captain unload the cedar, instead of arresting us all? *What* is so important about me, or my damn ship, that you're trying to negotiate? I'm not the King of Thailand. I'm a grubby pretend art restorer who grew up under communism and can smell a rat a galaxy away. So, don't play with me. And give me back my goddamned righteous anger. I've earned it."

Neither Markin Kelm nor the strange biped moved, but suddenly Yorden's nails were scrabbling the wood again and his teeth were grinding against each other. He no longer gave a damn about information, either, but the contract the markin had offered still looked real lucrative.

"We need someone to haul living andal. You are an opportunity."

"I am a criminal." Because he *was* a criminal, if a petty one, and it didn't bother him. Yorden relished the spittle that flicked from his lips as he spoke. The feeling of wanting to punch the markin returned. Excellent.

Anyway, his life had been shit and he was doing something about it, damn it, not just whining on Earth and embracing peace while working at a fast-print shop. If that meant a little crime, so what? At least it got him food. He could go back, he supposed. Go back to that Gaza settlement and the graves. Go back to Poland, which, to be fair, was a lot better now, but be haunted by childhood ghosts all the same. He could go somewhere new—the USA, maybe, or Canada—start over in whatever job a middle-aged Jew could get without prior training. He could do that and just slowly fade from existence while that sticky blanket of peace covered his planet's history. *His* history.

Fuck that.

Again, Kelm growl-sighed. "You are paranoid. Peace came because sentients everywhere strive for peace. It is an inevitability. You have no history of major crime, merely of being exposed to it, which leads me to believe your actions were born out of desperation, not malice. Your ship fits our needs, and we pay better than the black market. We need those trees, Captain. Play your games and destroy your world—destroy your solar system if you like—but we need those trees. As long as whatever you do doesn't affect Neek or Risal, we don't care."

Well, that was...a thing. Yorden swallowed his wonderment and sat back. "You're giving me release to do basically whatever I want as long as I move andal for you?"

Kelm tilted hir head. "More or less. Your application to take on a Journey youth is approved, and we've transferred four thousand diamond rounds for the safety upgrades needed to take on a child. So, go. Go back to your ship. There is andal waiting for transport presently on Neek. We would appreciate delivery within ten standard days and will pay, whatever your price."

There wasn't really anything more to say. What else was there to ask for? What else could he possibly want? He could do whatever he wanted, *be* whomever he wanted, and as long as those trees made it from point A to point B alive, well...damn. *Damn.* He'd have a teenager along for the ride, but still. *Damn.*

He signed the contract.

Yorden wanted to feel victorious, but as he stood and stalked from the room, too many questions danced in his head. The unease in his stomach wouldn't settle. The whole situation, from the happy beings here at the spaceport to the Risalian Markin Council all but begging for Yorden's help, spoke of...well, trouble. It was a deeper trouble than going weeks without meat or not being able to get a toy or even avoiding the fallout from the lethal squabbles over territory. Andal was a useful tool, but the Neek exported it by the shipload. Live trees versus dead ones shouldn't have made that much of a difference.

There was a secret here. There was a secret here that no one seemed to care about unraveling, and that made it all the more dangerous. Dangerous for him, but also dangerous for Earth and Mars and maybe the Neek people too, since they seemed to have some of the same unique quirks that Terrans did.

Yorden hated secrets about as much as he hated governments. If the Charted Systems were supposed to be his escape, then they were failing him already. He wouldn't be able to enjoy his time away from Earth until he knew what those secrets were. But maybe, just maybe, if he worked in the Systems long enough, did enough hauls for the Markin, they'd slip and he'd figure it out.

Or, he'd just have a lot of fun pissing them off.

Exile

220 AA

I have seen the barren forests! I've heard the voices of our scientists! We have to fight before our planet becomes a wasteland of fairy tales and woody detritus!

Snapping awake from her dream, Neek sucked in a chestful of air and nearly rolled out of her bedding. She blinked the room into focus, her eyes tight and dry from the rally last night, and her throat burned from all the yelling. She was planning another one for next week—well, her brother was, but she had every intention of going—but Neek tried, for once, to push politics from her mind.

She swallowed, cringing at the burn of spit on her dry throat, and pushed away her soft cotton blankets. Today, the andal failing, the deforestation of their old-growth forests, and the president's asinine policies could wait. Today, she would pretend to be a devout Neek. In a few hours—or a few minutes, depending on how late she'd slept—she and her family would leave for the ceremony marking her graduation from the Heaven Guard Academy, where Neek had taken top honors. Today was the day she officially moved out of the academy dorms and into a Heaven-Guard-sponsored apartment and began *real* pilot training. Whether there would be formal charges brought against her for the anti-government rally last night, or subsequent vandalism thereafter, it wouldn't matter in a few hours. In a few hours, she'd be untouchable.

"Are you coming down for breakfast?" her mother called from downstairs. "We need to leave soon!"

"Shit." Was it that late already? Neek grabbed the first pair of pants and shirt she saw on her floor, shoved them on, and then slammed her feet into her boots before quickly braiding her red-blonde hair. She took a minute to press *stuk*-covered fingers to a poster of a gleaming, crimson settee and her favorite Heaven Guard pilot dressed in the traditional golden robes piped with forest green.

"Soon," she whispered to the petite woman on the poster. "I'm going to be there soon."

"You going to meet Guard Four in that?" Neek's brother asked from the doorway.

"Huh?"

He came in, picked at the sleeve of her battered rayon shirt, and critically eyed her pants. "Your clothes. You can't go to graduation like that. You look like a Terran. Uncle will have a fit."

Neek huffed and batted her brother's hand away. His hair was a few shades darker than hers, his skin more ocher than copper, but no one would mistake either of them, even at a distance, for a Terran. Well, not unless they had never seen a Neek in person before. "No one cares what I wear underneath. The trainee silver robe will cover everything, and I want to be comfortable. You know those graduation speeches go on forever."

"And when they change your silver robe for gold?" her brother asked, his face turning smug. "When you sit in your trainee settee for the first time? This is what you want to be wearing?"

Neek frowned and ran a hand over her hair, tucking loose strands behind her ear. He had a point. She was hours from being in the Heaven Guard and having the freedom to fly wherever she wanted, to *be* whomever she wanted. Neek could fly her settee to the upper atmosphere of her homeworld and look out at the galaxy beyond filled with Risalians and Terrans and Minorans and so many others she had heard about but had never seen. She could even stay low to the ground and look at all the forests of Neek laid out before her—at the wilting leaves, the barren understories.

Neek's stomach turned. Even dying, the trees couldn't possibly care that her shirt was torn and that the hems of her pants weren't neatly tucked into the tops of her thick, brown boots. The trees—and the Heaven Guard, really—would care more about her *intent*, surely. She wouldn't be the heretic niece of the High Priest of Neek once she put on that gold robe. She wouldn't be Daughter from the Tertiary Forest Preserve. She would be Pilot, Heaven Guard Pilot, beholden only to the andal and a fantasy planet that didn't exist.

"Do I really need to change?" Neek muttered. She scuffed her boots against the floor. "What do you think?"

"I'll get you one of my high-necked shirts. A green one. It'll look amazing under both robes, and you won't look like a vagabond anymore." Her brother turned to leave, but Neek swatted at his shoulder.

"I look *fine*," she insisted. "I'm not dressing up for anything, not even the ceremony."

He clucked at her. "Not even for Guard Four, it appears. But hey, no violence now. Don't forget the most recent set of Charted Systems laws. You leave a bruise and they'll...I don't know. Lecture you to death or something."

Neek punched his shoulder, *hard*, for good measure.

Her brother laughed.

"The shirt won't fit. I stopped wearing your hand-me-downs last year. I'm taller than you, remember?"

Her brother tousled his curly, red hair and pursed his lips. "Yeah. Thanks for that reminder. Jerk."

Neek stuck out her tongue. That she was nineteen years old didn't matter. If her brother was going to act like a kid, then she was happy to meet him at his level—even if she had to duck down to reach it.

"I'm better at carving than you."

Neek snorted. "I'm better *looking* than you."

"Your girlfriend tell you that?"

"Did yours?"

"Children!" Neek's mother stormed into the room, took one look at Neek's clothes, and set her jaw. Her auburn hair hung limply, and although her clothes were clean and well pressed, they draped sharply from her shoulders, poorly concealing a thin frame. "*No.* Daughter, change. Son, stop." She shook her head and sighed. "Just...stop. We have to leave in ten minutes. Your talther and father are already in the land skiff."

"I didn't bring any other clothes," Neek said. "They're all back at the dorms."

Her mother produced a hacking cough. Neek's stomach twisted. How long had she been sick? Four months? Five? After the ceremony, after Neek had her robes, she'd take some time off. Help nurse her mother. Give the family a break.

"Then, go get something from your talther's closet. You two are about the same size. Meet your brother and me outside."

Her brother blew a raspberry at Neek before brushing past their mother and leaving Neek's childhood bedroom. Neek was about to follow, ready to punch him again, when her mother grabbed her wrist.

"Atalant." Her mother's voice was low. Dangerous.

Neek cringed at her child-name, at how demeaning it felt—today especially.

"Last night was too far," her mother warned, pulling her close. "You've made it about all of us."

"The riot wasn't planned. I had already stopped speaking by then."

"You think that means you won't be held responsible?"

Neek closed her eyes and took a deep breath. She didn't have the mental energy for this right now. "It'll be fine, Mother. No more until I'm Pilot. I promise. The family will be safe." Neek tried to soothe with her words, but her insides squirmed. She felt like a child being scolded for something she'd done just to get attention, instead of an adult who was desperately trying to save her planet and her people.

"You're naïve," her mother said.

"We can debate later. Shouldn't we get going?"

Her mother sighed and released her arm. "At least change your shirt."

Grumbling, Neek stalked from her room to the one her three parents shared, pulled the first tunic she saw from her talther's closet, and shoved it over her head, on top of the shirt she was already wearing.

"Hurry up!" her mother wheezed from the foot of the stairs.

Neek heard the door open and then caught the scent of trillium as it wafted up to the second floor of her house. For the briefest moment, she thought about running into the forest, hiding amongst the andal trunks as she had as a child, feeling thick moss between her toes, and bathing in a field of white petals. But it was only for a moment. She didn't have those dreams anymore, not since the first time she'd flown a ship. Not since her brother had bribed an engineer to get her a ride in a decommissioned settee. Not since she'd sat at the *stuk* interface and the natural secretions from her fingertips had linked her with the ship's outdated computer core.

Flight was what she wanted. A pilot was who she was. And nothing—not even the tempting smells of trillium flowers and andal sap—would keep her from her goal.

* * *

Crimson settees flew overhead in a perfect parabolic formation, pulling Neek's attention from the graduation speaker. Neek stood on a short podium, just a step ahead of the rest of her cohort, but she could still hear her roommate gasp as the small ships flew overhead. Neek's heart soared with them as her silver robe flapped against her legs. She wouldn't get her own settee at the end of this ceremony, but soon. She was first in her class, after all. Her flying had shattered every record, her timing and reflexes stupefying her professors. Master training would only be a formality, no doubt. A superficial step. She could pass the skills exam now if the academy would let her take it, but she doubted they would break the rules just for her. Still, she'd fulfill any stipulation, participate in any stupid ritual, to get into her own settee. She'd have a communal trainee ship in the meantime to practice in, and Neek knew that the moment her fingers hit the interface, the moment her *stuk* gelled into the cellulose biometal, she would fall in love.

"And now, I will introduce the graduates. Twenty in all—like the twenty years of the first *don*—but only ten will graduate to master class, and of those, perhaps two will receive permanent assignment to the Guard. Look upon their faces, dear family and friends. Our future stands before you."

The crowd cheered. Neek's parents and brother sat in the front row, their hands clasped to one another's, their faces beaming. The joy in Neek's chest burst across her face. Her *stuk* gelled.

Thank you, she mouthed to her brother. He frowned at her, seemingly confused, but it was him, after all, who had encouraged her to apply to the Heaven Guard. He had taught her to fly. To question. That she could calculate a *p*-value as well as she could turn a settee into a barrel roll was his doing. His patience. His guidance. This was her moment, but in some ways, it was her brother's, too.

"Daughter of the Tertiary Forest Preserve, N'lln, step forward and become Pilot."

The crowd fell into silence. Neek took two steps forward to the short gatoi who held a gold robe out to her, its hem, sleeves, and collar piped in green. She reached for the folded robe, let her gummy fingers grasp the fabric, and pulled it to her chest. It felt like touching a cloud, like if she loosened her grip even for a moment, the robe might condense and slip through her fingers. Her heart hammered in her chest, and she swore she could smell hints of trillium in the air, even though the academy was over an hour away from her parents' land.

"I've done it," she whispered to herself. Neek brought the fabric to her mouth and spoke into it. "It's finally done."

The gatoi moved behind her and began to unfasten the tiny metal hooks that ran the length of her silver robe. One by one, she felt the freed hooks loosen the fabric. She held the gold robe out in front of her. Smoothed the wrinkles away. Waited for the silver to pool at her feet so she could slide the cooling cotton over her head.

"End the tyranny of Ardulum!" a voice called from the crowd.

A rush of gasps sounded as Neek jerked her head up to scan the audience. The seats were mostly filled with family members, but at the sides and in the back, Neek were standing up. They wore simple clothes, not ceremonial ones or even formal dress gowns like the families. Neek saw clenched fists. She saw bruised faces and eyes looking at her with determination, hope, and *anger*.

"The Heaven Guard is a lie!" a man shouted from too-near the stage. "Ardulum is a lie! The president is a *lie!*"

Not here! Neek thought desperately. She tried to catch her brother's eyes, but he wouldn't look at her. In fact, he was looking at everything *but* her—at the families, the protestors, her parents. He almost looked...guilty.

Brother! she thought wildly. *Did you do this?* She couldn't imagine it, and the possibility shredded her heart. *He* was the one who had been so adamant that she join the Guard. They both had plans for what they could accomplish once she was beyond the president's reach. This was counter to all of their goals.

The gatoi's hands had stilled near her waist. "Oh," zie whispered.

A golden skiff flashed in Neek's peripheral vision. She turned toward it, and whatever remnants of joy that had swelled inside her only moments before burst and leaked from her with her thinning *stuk*. A hundred or so protestors could be dealt with. This...

"No," she whispered to herself. Because it couldn't be. The president of Neek had no business at a Heaven Guard ceremony. There were other gold skiffs on her planet. Perhaps it was someone's parents, arriving late. Perhaps a dignitary from another planet had made an unexpected visit. Perhaps one of the Cell-Tal board members—a Risalian cellulose engineer—was on-planet and wanted to see the ceremony. Either way, there were other possibilities. It wasn't going to be the president. He had no right to be here, protestors or no! The Guard belonged to the high priest. The Guard belonged to the Ardulan religion. On her world, Ardulum was greater than the president.

He has no right to be here!

The skiff landed just beside the stage, its repulsors burning the sedge. Its engine whine faded. The skiff's door opened, and Neek stopped breathing. Her heartbeat turned erratic. The President of Neek stepped from the ship. No *stuk* dripped from his fingers, which might have given Neek a hint to his mood. His curls were slicked back, and his face was so impassive that Neek wanted to slap him.

The protestors sat down. The families quieted. The president seldom left his governmental offices, and for all their rallies, Neek doubted that any of the people out in the crowd would dare insult the president to his face. He had bribed and manipulated his way into almost every aspect of society, had too much power over their world. Even the Heaven Guard trainees kept rigidly still. They'd not yet graduated. To leave the stage now would be to leave the Guard.

After him came four Old Family guards, dressed in what looked like riot gear. Neek had only seen pictures of such outfits. There was no call for that kind of clothing, not with the Charted Systems' omnipresent peace. Not even to deal with protestors who might have also been involved in some property destruction last night. No one got *hurt*, after all.

Neek stepped to the very edge of the stage and held her hands out. "Don't," she said. Her hands shook. This wasn't the time. This wasn't the place. He could be angry at her for the rallies and protests, or the editorial she'd gotten published in the *Neek Journal of Science & Technology* just a few days ago, but they could sort that later. That was for behind closed doors—a visit to her parents' house or an ambush at the temple. Not *here*.

But they didn't stop. Two guards grabbed her arms while a third grabbed fistfuls of her robe and ripped the silver fabric from her body. Dozens of protestors and no one said a thing. She let go of her gold robe, and it fell to her feet.

The president approached her, eyes hard.

"Stop!" she screamed, jerking her arms against the guards' hold. "You have no right to be here! Coward! You're as inept at timing as you are at leading!" Tears stung her eyes. Everyone was so silent. Her roommate. Her parents. Her brother, watching her with infuriating calmness. Even the damned people that were brave enough to damage an innocent person's stall but apparently couldn't be bothered to even speak up against *actual physical violence.*

"You wanted my attention." The president's voice was cool and calm. He stroked her cheek with dry fingers. "You have it. Unfortunately, you no longer have a place here. No place among us." He pointed to the crowd. "Look at what you cause, what you bring to a holy ceremony."

"Bastard!" she hissed at him. He wasn't special, was just as soft and sticky as any Neek. There was no reason to be afraid of him, strong-arm tactics notwithstanding. "This wasn't me. And you coming here, it will be all over the feeds. It will only boost our message further!"

The president's hand fell away. Again, Neek pulled at her captors, but their grips were firm and their *stuk* gelled, holding her even more tightly. They dragged Neek off the stage, her boots tearing at the sedge.

"My robe!" As they pulled her forward, Neek looked over her shoulder at the torn silver and trampled gold. "My *robe!*"

"Exiles don't wear robes," the president said in his syrupy voice. "Put her inside."

Neek's parents did scream, then, as the guards picked her up and threw her inside the skiff. Her palms tore as she fell onto the coarse biometal floor. She cursed—cursed Ardulum, the president, her uncle, the silent crowd, the failing andal plantations, and the old religion that would destroy her planet in another generation.

"She's our daughter!" Neek heard her father plea.

"She's the niece of the high priest!" That was her talther. Neek heard coughing, too. That was her mother. Neek's stomach twisted, and she scrambled to her feet.

"She is nothing, anymore," the president responded. "She is Exile."

"You can't!" Neek burst toward the door just as it slammed closed. She rebounded and fell back to the floor, her tailbone taking the brunt of the fall. The ship's engines began to whine, and the floor jostled as the craft left the surface.

Neek ran to the controls and slammed her hands on the *stuk* interface. Through the viewscreen, she saw capital buildings, the Ardulan Temple, and then treetops as the skiff left the city and moved to the suburbs. She tapped command after command into the computer, but each try brought an angry beep and no change in course. The ship was on autopilot and password locked. She had no control.

Neek swallowed, trying to ease the ache in her throat. Wherever they stashed her, she would find a comm. She would smuggle out handwritten messages if she had to. She wasn't going to give up. That she had lost the robes, lost the Guard...she could mourn that in time. Saving the forests, that was her job. Helping her people move beyond Ardulum so they could truly participate in the Charted Systems, that was why she did all this, right? That she loved piloting was just a bonus.

Right?

A low tremble went through the ship. Neek had never felt a skiff do that before. Had she lucked out? Was it malfunctioning? Neek sent another query to the computer. The ship was...

Neek blinked. It couldn't be.

The ship was going *up*.

Neek frantically queried the computer. The viewscreen still showed treetops, but that silo in the distance...that had been there the first time she'd looked. It had seemed closer for a while, but now, she realized as she squinted, it was far away again. She was watching a prerecorded loop!

"No!" The skiff was clearly going up. Neek's ears were popping, and there was a funny feeling in her gut. Her planet's skiffs were not designed to leave even the lower atmosphere. Only settees could do that, and this was no settee. Whatever the president's engineers had done to make it spaceworthy, it hadn't been nearly enough.

Neek threw commands at the computer. *Land. Coast. Glide. STOP.* Each returned with a ping and the perpetual image of treetops. He couldn't do this. He had no right to do this! What in Ardulum's name was the president thinking? Neek pounded at the controls, and the recorded loop fuzzed out to reveal space. Endless space.

Text scrolled across the computer screen:

Hours of air left: 233
Gallons of water remaining: 2
Food rations available: none
Communication systems: disabled
Destination: high orbit around planet Neek
Entertainment options: one video available of Heaven Guard airshow #4194, highlighting the double barrel rolls of Guard Four; all Neek holy texts available

Neek screamed. She kicked the console, her boot denting the cheap biometal. The Neek did *not* leave their planet. They did not live on space stations or strange worlds. They stayed put, to wait for Ardulum's return. And she...she was meant to *rot* up here, in Neek space—rot while watching a planet she could see but never again touch. Rot while the Heaven Guard executed flawless formations in Neek's upper atmosphere, ignoring her gold coffin spinning by. Rot while reading texts she'd had shoved down her throat since she was old enough to read—texts that were slowly destroying her planet.

And...and...

She would never get her settee.

She was only nineteen years old, and she was going to die, alone, in space.

And there was nothing she could do.

* * *

Her room smelled like silage. It should have smelled like wood, because her mother had just installed a new andal wardrobe and hadn't had time to varnish it, but this smelled...unattractive. Maybe something had curled up and died in the walls?

Hesitantly, she opened her eyes. She saw hock spurs. Brown hair. Cleft hooves.

She gasped in air, her chest too tight. She was surrounded by biometal and quadrupeds. She was no longer in her presidential coffin with the oxygen going so low that she couldn't stay awake. She was dead, surely. She was dead, and her soul hadn't made it to Ardulum because she was a heretical nonbeliever but apparently believed enough in the Minorans to end up in their afterlife instead.

That made complete sense.

"Do'ya have something to eat?" Neek croaked from her dry throat. Were you supposed to be hungry in the afterlife? Then again, what did she know? She hadn't expected death to smell so much like plant decay, either.

"She's awake." A Minoran knelt down onto the soft cushion Neek was curled into and nudged her nose at Neek's shoulder as she spoke in a clunky approximation of the Neek language. "Your uncle wishes you well, young Neek."

Neek blinked. "Can comms pick up prayers or something? Am I dead?"

The Minoran's ear twitched. "You're not dead. You're rescued. And your uncle asked us to give you this."

Another Minoran dropped a biofilm on the ground next to Neek. A faulty one, apparently, since it rolled in on itself instead of lying flat in its plastic scaffold. Neek just stared at it, trying to wrap her mind around being *alive* in a stinky Minoran ship instead of being *dead* in a stinky Minoran afterlife.

"It's a Neek-to-Common translation guide," the first Minoran said. "You'll need it. We've almost arrived."

A yawn overtook Neek as she pushed herself into a sitting position and crammed the crappy biofilm into her pocket. Alive. Huh. Everything around her still felt fuzzy, and she definitely sensed a headache coming on. Still, it did give her hope that at least someone in her family knew the president had tried to kill her. If her luck hadn't run out, then this ship would be landing on her homeworld and she'd be able to address the whole situation in person. Loudly. Hopefully with a crowd.

The kneeling Minoran stood just as the ship shook. Neek rose on wobbly feet and followed the Minoran—at least she assumed that was what the tail swishing indicated she do—out a gate-like door to a very definitive ship hatch. Usually, this close to a hatch, the air filters started pulling in native air—assuming it was breathable—to prepare the crew for the temperature and smells that were about to hit them. Smells were definitely crawling toward Neek, but they were rich and salty, not...mossy, which was the best way she could describe the smell of her planet.

"Wait," Neek said, putting her hand on the Minoran's shoulder. Her stomach twisted. "Where are we?"

The hatch opened, and Neek's headache hit. Everything was a blur of color and action. Pheromones and body odors assaulted her nose. There was screaming, screeching, the sound of metal on metal, as well as flesh—unwashed flesh—brushing and nudging and pounding into every surface.

She was led to the bottom of the ramp before she realized what had happened. The Minoran who had nudged her there clomped back up the biometal walkway—and the damn thing immediately began to retract.

"Wait!" Neek tried to jump to reach the receding edge of the walkway, missed by a hair, and fell onto her knees, ripping the thin fabric of her pants. Her mind spun. Her hands tingled. What was happening? Who were all these beings? How many languages was she hearing? Three? Ten?

"Where am I?" she yelled up, her voice squeaking.

"Callis Spaceport," the Minoran said. Over the yelling and haggling and shouting, Neek thought she might have caught the faintest bit of sadness in the Minoran's voice. Or, maybe she just wanted there to be some emotion in this exchange, for while she was glad she wasn't dead, being abandoned in a spaceport where she didn't speak the language wasn't much better.

"My uncle!" she tried one last time. "Please, if I could just—"

The hatch closed. The warning lights in the bay flashed, indicating imminent departure. Someone with long claws pulled her back from the ship, behind a blue, painted line, as its repulsors engaged. Her head thumped along with the rhythm of the crowd. Her *stuk* burned with the heat from the thrusters. And finally, she watched the last connection she had to her home fly into silver-spotted darkness, leaving her alone.

Again.

* * *

Neek stood in the center of a five-way intersection at what felt like the middle of the spaceport, but was probably just a small artery, and gawked. She needed food, and she desperately wanted to find a comm to call home, but she had no idea where to start with either problem. Andal help her, she didn't even know what half these beings *were*, much less how to talk to any of them.

What the hell was she supposed to do in a spaceport? Beg? Wander around until someone took pity on her and gave her a piloting job?

In the back of her mind, the childish part, Neek had hoped the Minorans would have given her a few diamond rounds to get by, or a tip about where to find a job, or even just a friendly parting smile. Rotting andal, they could have let her use their damn comm! She had *nothing* except her tattered clothes, the translating biofilm, and a bunch of emotions she wanted to bury. Thousands of beings swarmed around her, their arms brushing hers, their hair in her face, their hooves and claws clipping her boots, and all Neek could do was stand there and think about that stupid Heaven Guard video the president had uploaded to the skiff. Now, she didn't even have that. All she wanted was to curl up in her mother's arms and be told that everything was going to work out. At the very least, she wanted the chance to say goodbye.

Goodbyes meant finding a comm though, and chances were that comms took currency of some sort. Neek, of course, had none, nor did she speak much Common. She'd taken one course at the Heaven Guard Academy. It hadn't been a required class, and why should it have been, given that no one ever left the planet? She spoke her planet's primary dialect and the one from her province, but neither were going to be helpful out here, especially not if she was trying to find a job.

So, she covered her nose against the utterly incomparable smell of thousands of beings and tried to make a decision. Turn right? Turn left? Head forward? Follow the green sign with some sort of aquatic animal on it and words she couldn't read, or follow the yellow sign with a distinct image of fast-print cellulose perf?

Neek's stomach growled. She had to choose. A plan would be best. It would mean that Neek wasn't adrift in a tide of flesh, just that she was merely getting her bearings. Right? Who needed a settee or gold robes when one was in the biggest spaceport in the Charted Systems? She'd find some fast-print shop, grab leftovers from one of the tables, wash them down with her pride, and then go from there.

Neek took a step into the crowd toward the yellow perf sign, her Neek-to-Common biofilm tucked into the pocket of her pants. She had enough Common to get herself into trouble. Wonderful. Maybe someone would have an antique gun and just shoot her in the head.

A Risalian in a blue tunic walked into her.

Neek lost her balance.

The Risalian's claws, perhaps grabbing her shirt to steady her, instead ripped the fabric and spun her a quarter turn before she hit the floor. She had tried to grab something on her way down but had managed only to glide off the bare arm of a gigantic Terran. Her elbow took the brunt of the impact, and Neek cursed Ardulum as her head was kicked by a pair of feet. No one except for her was wearing footwear. That didn't make any sense at all. Was she finally full-on hallucinating from oxygen deprivation and the lack of food?

Beings chided her in languages she didn't understand. The Terran she'd covered in *stuk* was staring at her with what looked like fascinated disgust. Neek frowned and made a shooing motion, like he was some gigantic, hairy insect. "You're not so hot-looking yourself, you know," Neek muttered. "Got enough arm hair to be mistaken for an Alusian, and it looks like a small animal has taken residence on your face."

That was all in Neek, of course, but the Terran was studying her now, like he was contemplating her words.

"Jeez, buddy. Never seen a Neek before? Don't you read?"

The Terran chuckled.

"Come," a voice said in Common. That voice was much higher pitched, and it didn't belong to the Terran.

Neek pivoted on her hip. The Risalian she'd run into reached out and helped her stand. His black hair was loosely braided down his back, and his blue skin looked pasty in the artificial light. He was only wearing a blue tunic made of what looked like rayon, pressed and sharp. As he breathed, the gill slits in his neck flapped open and shut with a little *wisp* sound that made Neek feel vaguely seasick. Why was he... Wait, no, not a he. Neek chided herself. Risalians had one sex and reproduced through budding. Their pronouns in Common were...argh! She couldn't remember. It? No, that wasn't right. Xe maybe? Not zie though—that was for sure a third-gender pronoun. She'd have to ask directly and hope the Risalian wouldn't take offense.

"My Common is bad," Neek said in Common—the one phrase she'd made sure to memorize—as the Risalian led her through the crowd to a small seating plaza. Colorful flowers grew under an artificial sun lamp. What with the walls and floor of the station all a uniform pale brown, it was a welcome change. Neek even heard the sound of flowing water, although none was apparent. "Your...not name. Your small name. You're...not 'he,' not 'she.' What?"

The Risalian's neck slits flushed purple. "Xe...and hir," the Risalian said and then motioned for her to sit.

Well, she was offending beings already. Great start to her first week as Exile.

"Sit," xe ordered.

"Food?" Neek asked hopefully, her stomach growling again. "Job for a wayward Neek, which pays in advance and provides comm access?" she added in her native tongue.

"*Sit.*"

What else was she going to do? Run off? Neek sat.

The Risalian squinted at her and rubbed hir neck slits. The Common words came slowly then, each well enunciated. "You walk without thinking. Why are you here? Are you lost? Do you...belong here?"

Neek pursed her lips. Really? Xe was irritated with *her*? She wasn't the one who'd done the pushing. And her presence wasn't that unusual. Neek were members of the Charted Systems. Just because her people chose not to leave the planet didn't mean they weren't a fully participating entity. She had the same right to be here as anyone else.

"Are you Alusian?"

"Are my arms covered in fur?" Neek asked incredulously, forgetting to use Common. "Do your eyes work?"

Apparently, her tone didn't need translating. "Terran?" the Risalian countered.

That, at least, was a reasonable mistake. Terrans had a lot more phenotypes than the Neek, but they both had a lot less hair than Alusians and their skin didn't run into the blue spectrum like the Risalians'. "Neek," she said, pointing to her chest. "Job?" she added in Common, because if she was already a spectacle, then she might as well get something out of it.

The Risalian spouted a fast string of words in response, none of which Neek understood.

"Neek," she said again. This time, she held up a hand and splayed out her fingers. She had eight per hand, like most Neek, and the *stuk* glistened in the fake sunlight.

Xe opened hir eyes wide and nodded in understanding. "Neek," xe repeated. Xe pointed to hir own chest. "Kelm."

Neek frowned. A blue tunic on a Risalian, not quite the same color as their skin, signified something. Governing body? Cell-Tal? She couldn't remember. She knew that Risalians were bipeds with an aquatic lineage, hence their lithe frames and the gill slits in their necks. Everything else was a little hazy. They had only one inhabited planet. Maybe. Maybe a moon or two, as well. They oversaw the Charted Systems' peace—she was sure of that—which was why this one was hovering over her like she was some distraught child.

Kelm said another garbled sentence and pointed at the hallway to Neek's left. Several neon signs hung suspended from the ceiling, flashing in pink and orange. The mass of colors and blinking lights and characters she didn't recognize made her head hurt. Neek followed Kelm's finger to a pale green one that had four words on it, one of which was "child."

"I'm not a child," Neek said acerbically, forgetting to use Common again. "And I'm not lost. I need a job, and I need food, not necessarily in that order."

Kelm gave her a tried look. Neek really, really wanted to smack hir in the neck slits. Instead, she took a deep breath and said in Common, "No child. Adult."

Kelm laughed and again pointed down the hall. This time, xe spoke slowly, enunciating each syllable.

Neek pursed her lips. Memories tumbled in her head for a few moments as she tried to recall how the Systems dealt with childcare or even orphaned children. What did they do with vagrants of any age? *Were* there vagrants in the Charted Systems? Hadn't poverty gone away when crime had—or had it been the other way around? Who would just be wandering...

"Withering andal. No. I am *not* a Journey youth." Her Common disintegrated as her temper flared hot. "I don't need two years of guided wandering set up to teach kids how to act like competent adults. I *am* an adult. I've finished my education. I graduated with top honors from the Heaven Guard Academy. I've been through every form of apprenticeship and training I will ever need. I've had a gold robe *in my hands*. I know where my life is going, I'm on track...sort of, more or less, and I don't need your— your *guidance*. I've had enough well-meaning oversight to last me a lifetime. You can take your asinine cultural exchange program for teenaged symbionts and shove it through your neck slits. Some of us take real jobs when we become adults, instead of going on a two-year vacation around the Systems. Some of us are perfectly capable of taking care of ourselves!"

Kelm tapped a claw against hir mouth.

Neek growled, bunched her hands into fists, and tried again in Common. "Adult! Pilot! Adult!"

"Identification." Kelm held out hir hand expectantly. Neek cursed again. She knew that word well, but of course she didn't have any on her. The president had made sure of that. Bodies orbiting in space didn't need identification when they were sealed up in a golden coffin.

"Neek adult fifteen rotations!"

Kelm exhaled through hir lung slits and shook hir head. Again, hir words came slowly and clearly. "Eighteen old enough to leave with guide. No guide, only Youth Journey. At twenty, apprenticeship. At twenty-one, free travel. How old are you?"

"No." Neek wanted to yell that it was none of Kelm's business, but she didn't know how to say that in Common, and it technically *was* Kelm's business. But she'd be damned if she was going to be babysat for the next year, and Ardulum could fuck any apprenticeship. She'd become an apprentice pilot when she was ten. She was a damned adult. If she was adult enough to get kicked off her homeworld, then she was adult enough for the Systems. She didn't need her failure, her exile, rubbed in her face constantly for the next year by being forced through some mentorship program for *children*. She needed food, and she needed access to a comm. She did *not* need this.

"How old?"

"No!"

"How old?"

Neek tried to storm off back into the crowd of beings and well away from the brightly lit, little hostel that no doubt held eager, star-eyed teens from across the Charted Systems, but a clawed hand across her wrist held her back. Kelm stood, eyes dark and a stony expression across hir face. Neek caught sight of the bushy Terran slouching against a wall and watching the whole scene with amusement.

"How old?" Kelm asked again, with maddening calmness.

Neek jerked. Claws broke through the thin fabric of her talther's shirt, ripping it further.

Her talther's shirt.

Her family...

Neek's arm went slack. Her bluster bled away. Her *stuk* thinned. Aliens surrounded her, their smells and bodies and languages grotesque and wild, and the last part of her family lay shredded against her skin. She had nothing. She *was* nothing. Andal help her, she was supposed to have returned to her parent's home after the ceremony to help her talther slaughter a *titha* so they could have bacon in the morning. They had been planning on going hiking afterward—a big celebratory thing for her graduation. And now...*this*.

The *stuk* on her fingertips dried. Her body would reroute it into tears if she didn't get control of herself. She felt the tears gather anyway.

"How old?"

"Nineteen."

"Follow." Another clawed hand closed around Neek's upper arm, and she was half led, half dragged, around a group of carousing Terrans, a short Minoran, and a shimmering slick of *something* toward the cheerful, green neon sign. The gigantic Terran didn't follow, which was a shame, because Neek could have used someone to punch that wasn't an authority figure, although she'd be damned if she let *anyone* see her cry. Still, given the stains on his flightsuit, that half smirk on his face, and the way he was trying so hard to look nonchalant, he looked like the kind of guy that kept a few antique pistols around, just to piss off the galactic constabulary. Maybe if she wiped off her damn tears and just punched him, he would shoot her and then she'd have a quick death in a spaceport instead of a slow, maddening death by asinine teenaged conversation.

"Hey." Neek tugged against Kelm's grip. Hir claws tightened. "Hey!"

"You are to go here," xe said irritably. "Just walk."

"Given a choice between being a Journey youth and being pushed out an airlock, I choose the airlock." Her sentence was in Neek. She didn't care. At least her voice hadn't trembled despite her throat swelling with unbearable emotions about a family she'd never see again.

Kelm stopped moving long enough to scowl at her before pushing her through a flashing doorway into a brightly lit foyer filled with Charted Systems teens playing a kicking game with a ball.

"No choice," xe said firmly, in Neek's own language, before turning from her, exiting the hostel, and slamming the door behind hir.

* * *

"I got it."

"Turn another five degrees to starboard, Sticky. Otherwise, you'll break the back thrusters before you finish rotation. I thought you said the Neek went to junior pilot school or something. You fly like an Oori."

"I *said,* I got it." Neek ground her teeth and leaned into the console. Her *stuk* was already thin from irritation, so her fingers slipped across the bioplastic interface. The shuttle banked slightly to port.

The Alusian captain threw up her hands and stormed over to the console. "Clumsy, undereducated Neek! Just stop. Stop! I'll do it myself."

Neek continued rotating the ship. "I'm not clumsy, and I'm almost done. Just give me another few seconds."

"No, you're done!" The Alusian pushed Neek from the console. With a sneer, she used the sleeve of her long, white robe to wipe the console dry and then reentered a set of commands. The shuttle listed, and the hull thruster misfired. The ship banked into the wall and acquired a five-meter-long gash in its biometal.

Horrible, ear-piercing alarms blared throughout the docking bay. Neek backed away from the console and glared as the Alusian frantically tried to control the ship. Everything would have been fine if she just would have let her finish. She'd done the calculations three times: there'd been plenty of room. She'd flown land skiffs with half as much maneuverability, and through much smaller areas. A little trust, for once, would have been nice.

The shuttle jerked again and launched itself into the opposite wall. This time, the wall itself dented. "Your contract is terminated!" the Alusian screeched. "You are incompetent. No wonder you people never leave your planet!"

The shuttle finally smashed to the biometal floor, Neek barely keeping her balance where she stood. Outside, the sounds of thuds echoed throughout the hangar as Minoran plating fell from the hull of the ship.

With a curse, the Alusian slammed her fist against the console, releasing the lock on the exit hatch. As the gangplank descended to the hangar, Neek snarled, shoved her hands into the pockets of the Youth Journey coveralls she wore—mint green and far too snug across her hips— and stalked out of the ship and into the bay. She was most definitely not going to be paid for this job, especially as she'd only put in half a day's work. She hadn't been paid for her last job, either, since the gas leak she'd reported but had not *caused* had been blamed on her, nor the time before that, when the Terran shopkeeper had taken one look at her hands and demanded she leave the store.

The comm—the *pay* comm in the corner of the hostel— remained frustratingly out of reach.

She was about to turn toward the hostel—ready to spend the rest of the day staring at the bottom of the bunk above her, practicing the hand motions for settee drills and dreaming of all the vile curses she could hurl at the president when she could finally afford a comm—when an open bay door caught her attention. Neek was in the beta wing of the spaceport, which mostly housed single berths for the wealthier clientele, as well as for those who had something to hide. Doors weren't just left open.

Since the worst anyone could do was yell at her when she was wearing the ridiculous Journey coveralls, Neek changed course and walked right in. Maybe she'd find a comm with a broken credit charger. Maybe she'd find a ship so beautiful that she'd forget she was stranded on a stinking space station—even if only for a moment.

An Oorin dredger sat in the center of the bay. Its massive, open hold had been recently cleaned. Neek could smell the disinfectant. There was heat coming off the plate armor, which meant it was likely getting ready to leave. Lost in thought, Neek toyed with the insignia on her coveralls, plucking at the stupid embroidered words. A steady rotation of Risalians checked up on her every night in the hostel. If she stowed away on the dredger, even if she was legitimately offered passage, they'd have her back in half a day in that moldy bunk with her Minoran and Terran roommates. But there'd be a general comm on the dredger. She could call home. She could talk to her parents and brother. She could just sneak on and use it. Quickly. No one would ever know.

"You lost?"

Neek jumped, feeling guilty despite herself. Wincing, she looked down. On the ground was a silvery puddle of...goop with a rectangular metal box floating on top. It looked like an old universal translator, which meant this was an Oori. That box would be their breathing apparatus, too, since the station was set up for oxygen breathers. There was a separate spaceport—a smaller one—near one of the other moons where the Oori did commerce with just each other.

"Just dreaming," Neek quickly replied. "I used to be a pilot." There was no particular reason to add the last part. Wistfulness would only bite her in the ass later.

"Can you pilot a dredger? My last pilot died."

Tone didn't really come through on a universal translator, so Neek had no way of knowing if that was supposed to have been a joke, a lament, or a warning. Still, her stomach fluttered. Piloting was a job a Journey youth could undertake, and it would get her off the station and away from Risalians. She'd be able to use the comm. It didn't even matter if the dredger was just going to one of Oorin's moons. She'd be *flying*.

"Why did the pilot die?"

"Methane poisoning. Hold had a leak. It's just done being repaired."

"Your comm work?"

"Yes, of course."

"Could I use it when off duty?"

The surface of the Oori rippled. "If you know how."

Neek huffed. "I had a standard education."

"Yes, but you are also a Neek."

Her face flushed, and her *stuk* became tacky. Yeah, she was a Neek. Yeah, they didn't use much technology. Yeah, they worshipped a planet that disappeared hundreds of years ago and probably never existed at all. Yeah, they were xenophobic, but they were still *her people.* With balled fists, Neek managed, "I know how to fly, and I know electronics. Neek aren't technologically inept. We just don't use them a lot. Do you want a pilot? I'm here, and I want off this station."

The Oori shimmered into an off-green tint. Their puddle body rolled in on itself, like the being was trying to make themselves into a drippy baguette. The translator box continued to float on top, although now it looked more like it was embedded in green putty than floating on a pool. "The job of a dredger pilot requires a waiver due to dangers."

Neek ground her teeth. "I don't care. I'd rather be poisoned than go back to that hostel. Are you registered with the Risalians? Can you sign the waiver for these 'dangers' and my paperwork?"

Bubbles foamed across the surface of the Oori. "I am registered. You're not my first Journey youth."

"The last one wasn't—"

"Systems law forbids you from being put in danger. My last pilot was...unlucky. The hold is fixed. I have the inspection paperwork. I can send a contract to the Youth Journey headquarters now. Processing the paperwork will take one day. You may familiarize yourself with the controls immediately."

A small animal was trying to fly out of Neek's chest. She needed her heart rate to slow down, her breathing to find a rhythm again. She needed her stomach to stop trying to jump through her throat. Three weeks in this dung heap of a spaceport, and this was the closest she'd ever come to having access to a comm. If it slipped through her *stuk*-covered fingers now, Neek didn't think she'd recover. "And the comm?"

One of the Oori's bubbles popped, and Neek was pretty certain it was supposed to be a laugh. "Yes, you may use the comm."

"And the contract?" Neek breathed. Her mouth was too dry. The sides of her pants were wet with *stuk*. "How long would the contract be for?"

"A year. A month. A week. I don't care. I need a pilot now. We can do week to week, if wanted."

She would have worked on one of the Oorin moons and worn an oxygen respirator for the next year if it meant getting at a comm and away from the Risalians. "Deal."

Three more bubbles burst near the edges of the rolled-up Oori. With the translator staying firmly on top, the being rolled to the bay door. They paused at the threshold and gave a very loud burp. Neek thought they might say something, but the Oori resumed rolling, eventually turning a corner.

Neek ran up the dredger's ramp, found the comm, and pounded in the call coordinates for her parent's home on Neek. When the computer asked for her identifier, she paused. You had to have one to make a call on most comms. She didn't know what to use. Had she been named Exile officially? If she typed "Daughter of the Tertiary Forest Preserve, N'lln," would the operators know who she was? She could use her child-name, maybe, as each was unique, but then the operator would have to dig through birth records. Neek had a small global population, all things considered, but it wasn't *that* small.

With heavy hands—her *stuk* all but absent thanks to the damn tears she couldn't quite keep under control no matter what she tried—Neek typed in "Exile" and initiated the call. It was hard to breathe. It was hard to think. Her coveralls were too tight on her hips and too loose on her shoulders, and her dry feet itched inside her boots.

Answer, she begged silently. *Please answer.*

A sloshing sound came from the comm. Text scrolled past in Common, too fast for Neek to read properly. She tried again. Again, the sloshing sound.

Her mouth was too dry. Her tongue felt like swollen sandpaper. More slowly this time, Neek keyed in the code for her brother's personal comm. *Come on*, titha *breeder. Answer your comm.*

Sloshing.

Neek's stomach rolled. She felt both empty and heavy. Her hands trembled, and the tears threatening to spill made her feel like she was a toddler having a tantrum. She'd been so patient. She'd taken all those dead-end jobs and put up with all those thinly veiled insults about her homeworld, her *stuk,* her exile, and her religion just to get to a comm, and now...now this?! Neek ran through the numbers of everyone she knew. Her mother. Her father. Her talther. She tried the planet's central comm. She tried the diplomatic channels, the open channels, the trade channels... Everything came back with the same nonresponse.

Neek slammed her palm against the comm and bit the inside of her cheek. The pain would keep the tears from coming. She was too old to cry. She knew what exile meant. Abstractly, she knew, but it still felt like the methane in the dredger hadn't been filtered out. No matter how hard she breathed, Neek couldn't fill her lungs. All she could hear was the sloshing, the sound of a rejected call. She didn't exist to her people anymore. She couldn't go home, and she couldn't call home—and how in Ardulum's name was she supposed to move *forward* when everything she had ever loved, and everything that had ever meant a damn to her, was locked away? Was she supposed to stay on this stupid station forever, surrounded by smelly aliens and incompetent pilots?

The comm pinged.

Neek forced herself to exhale. She rubbed her eyes, hoping that it would take away the black spots from her vision. The comm pinged again. Common scrolled across the screen, but this time, Neek caught the characters for her name: Exile, in big silvery font, followed by more incomprehensible Common.

It was enough. Neek accepted the call. There was a fluttering in her chest as hope rose from the twisting, shameful realizations that if only she had skipped that last rally, if only the other protestors hadn't resorted to property damage, if only, if only, *if only...*

The face of Neek's father filled the screen. Well, the face of her father with white hair instead of silver and a constellation of freckles across the nose that her father lacked. His skin was the same copper color as Neek's, and they had the same high cheekbones. The man wore a golden robe with ruffles instead of the colored piping of the Heaven Guard robes, and he had the look of practiced serenity that had always made Neek want to throw something at him, just to see if he could emote at all.

"Neek." Her uncle nodded and smiled tightly. That he'd chosen the common name over her official one was a kindness, but not one that she wanted from him.

"Uncle," Neek managed to choke out. "High Priest."

"You are well?"

Neek blinked. Anger rose too quickly and spilled out into her words. "I'd have *died* in that skiff without the Minorans. He meant to kill me!"

"But he didn't."

"Because you intervened!"

"Yes, I did. It's what Ardulum would have wanted."

Neek bit back a scream. "Uncle!" Neek pressed closer to the screen. "Forget Ardulum. I have to come home. I have to see my parents. I have to talk to my brother. Can you help me? Please? That's what you do, isn't it? Help people?"

Her uncle's lips pursed. He shifted in his seat, and in the background above him, near the top of the screen, she could see a gold robe piped with green. And then, another one. And another.

"Why are they here?" Neek whispered as her face flushed.

"To remind you of what you've lost, I'd assume. The president isn't subtle. Ignore them."

But Neek couldn't ignore them. She could only see up to their waists, but she'd spent enough time staring at the posters in her bedroom to identify footwear. The guard on the left was Guard One, the leader of the current squadron whose record time around N'lln Neek had shattered her first official day in a settee. Next to him was Guard Six, her strapped sandals and slight pigeon toe bringing a smile to Neek's face despite the mortification that was building inside her. Building, because Neek knew who was standing on the right, without even looking. The president would not have missed the chance to include Guard Four, Neek's personal idol. Sure enough, when Neek looked, there were the telltale knee-high leather boots, similar to the ones she wore. The clasped hands in front of the golden robe had golden nails, and the pilot's skin was the same deep copper as Neek's.

My humiliation wasn't complete, Neek thought as she wiped her fingers on her legs and swallowed the lump in her throat. *It wasn't complete until just now. Even if I got to go back, even if the president lifted my exile, how could I ever look any of the Heaven Guard in the eyes again?*

"Neek?"

Neek looked back at her uncle. There was some part of her that still cared about what he had to say, surely. Her wounds were deep, but he could always cut deeper.

Her uncle reached down and came back up with a rigid, transparent biofilm, which he tapped against his armrest. "Neek, pay attention. I've reached a deal with our president that could result in your repatriation, assuming key tenets are met.”

“Key tenets...” Neek blindly repeated. Over her uncle’s shoulder, she could still see the mix of green and gold. She should have been there with them, standing with them, *flying* with them. What did her shame taste like to the Guard? Were any of her cohorts there too, remembering the late-night agility drills, the early-morning mechanical maintenance, the camaraderie of belonging to the most elite group on Neek?

“Are you listening to me?”

“No,” Neek said flatly. “What do I have to do to be allowed back? Keep my mouth shut? Allow our world to be destroyed?”

Her uncle chuckled and opened the biofilm. Text in Neek scrolled across it in thick segments. “No, Neek. You could start, though, by telling me what you know about Ardulum.”

Where she had been too hot a moment before, now she was too cold. Where her rage had boiled, now her insides felt frozen. He had to be kidding. She believed in Ardulum as much as she believed in the President of Neek being a decent ruler. She’d spent her life running from religious services. There was no way she was sitting through them now without the promise of the Heaven Guard to keep her in line.

“What do I have to do to come home?” she asked again through clenched teeth.

Her uncle placed the biofilm down and folded his hands. “Not as much as you might think. You will speak weekly with me—and no one else. You will have no contact with anyone from our homeworld. When I deem you in an appropriate state to return, these restrictions will be lifted.”

“And what is that state?” Neek spat out.

Once more, her uncle held up the biofilm, *The Book of the Arrival* plastered widely across its surface.

Neek slammed her hand against the console and terminated the connection.

Just a Bar on Mars

2050 CE

Well, he was fucked. There weren't any other words for it.

The Cell-Tal computer had seemed like an amazing idea at the time, especially since it wasn't like he'd had to *pay* for it, but this was one scheme Yorden definitely had not thought through.

His Buran shuttle was the age of dirt. Its last pilot had probably been a dinosaur. And yeah, it *worked*, in the way a toaster with a broken lever still worked if you pulled the toast out with a set of tongs, but he was now short a metaphorical pair of tongs. The *Pledge* was too old to completely give up manual control—as it was still routed through the very amusing yoke he'd installed—but now seventy-five percent of navigation went through the new computer. This meant he had to work both a yoke *and* a computer simultaneously to fly the damn thing, and Yorden was a big man with big hands, but he'd need a damn octopus to get the *Pledge* off the ground again.

So, he was out hunting.

Well, he was also drinking. And eating. And sitting. Hunting could be done in a cushioned chair if you were the "shooting fish in a barrel" type, and he wasn't at his favorite bar on Mars by accident. A certain Oorin dredger had landed at Isidis Port just a few days after his computer installation, and the serendipity, the blind *luck,* was a little too much to pass up. And so, what he'd planned as just a general Youth Journey offer was about to turn into a pilot job. He hoped. Not that he was the stalker type, but Yorden couldn't just ignore the scared teen he'd seen at Callis a few months back. He hadn't known what to do with her then, or how to help, but damned if the universe wasn't aligned in their favor. He hated Risalians—she hated Risalians. Neither of them had a home to speak of. They both chafed at rules, and while Yorden doubted the Neek would take charity, he knew she'd take a job. Especially a job like this.

So, Yorden sat in his favorite chair—with the carved wood armrests and sturdy back support—and half played a game of blackjack with a few other tramp captains, all while keeping an eye on the Neek glaring down at the bar counter. He was just close enough to hear the conversation.

"How are you going to pay for that?" The bartender—a human with thick, black hair, brown skin, and dimpled cheeks—tapped the countertop.

"No money," Neek responded, refusing to make eye contact. Yorden knew how much the whole Journey youth thing inflamed her, but if she was short on credits, then his offer would be her only out. Oh, but she'd make it as painful as possible first—he was certain of it. She wasn't even wearing the telltale green coveralls, and she had her hands on her lap, hiding them under the bar.

"No money?" the Terran asked incredulously.

"No," she mumbled.

Yorden saw *stuk* flake onto the floor and shook his head. Stubborn as all hell, even after four months on a dredger—which also explained *why* she'd stayed on said dredger, despite Oorin food tasting like *titha* ass.

The bartender's voice softened. "How old are you, friend?"

"Hey, Kuebrich, you going to hit or what?"

Yorden shook his head, not bothering to look back at the table. He put his cards down and smoothed the top of his beard away from his eyes. The gambling at the bar counter was far more interesting. The Neek could lie and get herself arrested for not paying, or she could tell the truth and watch the bar mutate around her. While Yorden valued a good liar, seeing how she dealt with what was sure to be a...loud situation was also of interest.

Flaked *stuk* drifted from Neek's ears. "I'm a pilot, you know."

Yorden nodded to himself. *He* knew that quite well. He knew about her skill, her awards, her exile. You didn't make as many runs to Neek as he did for the Risalian Markin Council and not catch the gossip. The bartender, on the other hand, just looked confused.

"Friend? How old?"

Neek mumbled, "*Titha* crap. I'm nineteen."

"Then, it's on the house."

Yorden watched Neek redden from the tips of her ears all the way down to her neck. She managed a garbled "thank you" as she pulled the glass toward her and sipped the contents, her eyes still on the counter.

"Fatal mistake there," Yorden whispered, not intending for Neek to hear. "Look what you've done with your fingers."

The bartender perked up the moment Neek put the cup back down, the incredible width of her palm seeming to unsheathe the cup rather than simply release it. This was the whole reason Yorden had thought of her for the pilot gig in the first place. The Neek people had amazing hands but were as passive as any other Charted Systems automaton. But this Neek...ah, this one he'd seen in action. Hell, he'd read the Risalian reports. Given any agency at all, she'd burn the Charted Systems to the ground.

Yorden loved that idea.

"You're a long way from home!" the bartender exclaimed.

Neek growled in the back of her throat, which had to have been unnerving for the bartender, especially since Yorden could hear it clear across the bar.

"You're pretty articulate, you know, all things considered," the bartender said, unphased.

Neek's head flew up, and the redness faded from her face. "Please stop patronizing me."

The bartender shook her head and then smiled the most bullshit, condescending smile Yorden had ever seen. Hell, *he* was ready to punch the woman.

"Common must be really hard for you, huh? The Oori have tech to get around the language issue, but if Neek mouths aren't evolved like ours, and your tech is behind...wow. You must really have it rough."

"No, the bar floor is rough, and if you don't stop talking, I'm going to rub your face across it."

This time, Yorden had to stifle a laugh. Neek had said that last line in her native language, which Yorden spoke quite fluently. God help him, she was going to be perfect.

"Can I get you another drink, friend?" the bartender asked with a grin.

Neek switched back to Common and forced a smile. "Yes, thank you. That would be gloriously, beautifully lovely."

The bartender patted Neek on the shoulder before picking up her cup primly by the rim—so as to not touch the residual *stuk*, Yorden supposed—and disappearing behind a swinging wooden door. Yorden watched Neek's jaw set as she silently seethed. This was the hardest part. When to approach? If she were in a good mood, then she'd have no reason to sign on with him, although Yorden couldn't imagine a dredger being at all fun to fly. If she were in a spiteful mood, she'd just as likely dismiss him, and that would ruin further chances.

Still, if he could get two sentences in, he knew he could hook her interest. He had the only non-Risalian ship that had clearance to land on the Neek planet. If she was looking to visit home, get away from the taunts and jabs and glares of the Charted Systems, then he was her best option. The problem was getting those two sentences *in* while dealing with a being who was as prickly as Yorden himself.

The bartender returned—hands reddish from what Yorden assumed was a thorough scrubbing—sat another cup of the fizzy pink drink in front of Neek, and bustled away, an awkward smile plastered to her face.

"Captain Kuebrich, you in for another round, or you just going to daydream all day?"

"Huh?" Yorden forced himself to turn around and engage with the two Terrans and the Minoran at his table. They were all men, which was boring as fuck as far as Yorden was concerned, but for whatever reason, that was how things went with tramp captains. Maybe women and other genders found better ways around the rules. Maybe men just liked the smell of bars and barely legal crime. Maybe he just had too shallow a friend pool.

"Yeah, I'll go another round." He flipped six diamond rounds onto the table. "I think I'm going to bring another over, too, if you guys don't mind."

The Minoran's rear wiggled. "If they have rounds, I don't care." Both of the Terrans shrugged.

Right. Action then. Yorden sucked in some air tinged with the inevitable scent of multi-species BO and maneuvered to the bar, only to see that the inevitable had already occurred.

"Hey, there, gorgeous."

Yorden backed off a bit to reevaluate. A Terran with pale skin and yellow hair, in clothes that looked no better than Neek's, had leaned his elbow on the bar. Yorden was momentarily confused at how nonchalant the guy appeared—it's not like anyone in the Systems had experience picking up Neek—until he realized the suitor hadn't seen Neek's hands yet because they were crammed into her pants.

"Buy you another?" the man asked, tucking a springy, blond curl behind his ear. Yorden thought he might vomit.

Neek closed her eyes and appeared to curse under her breath. "I'm a Journey youth," she said, spitting the words.

Most beings, unfortunately for Neek, did not share the same level of disgust with the designation—nor did this one seem put off by the implications.

"I own a casino down the street. It's lovely to meet you. What are you drinking?" The man slid his very firm ass onto the stool next to Neek and managed to put together a smile that was nearly charming.

Yorden scratched his own ass through his thick, beige flightsuit and snorted. He'd been that young once, and that fit, but he'd always been a hell of a lot smoother with the ladies.

"No, thank you. I'm not interested. In anything." Neek tipped her glass up and finished the drink, her eight fingers splayed across the surface. Yorden choked on a laugh. By the time the cup hit the bar again, the suitor's face was incredulous.

"You're *her,* aren't you?" he asked, his jaw dropping so low that Yorden could have punched his fist into his mouth. "The Neek."

"Would you please go away?" Neek sighed and made a shooing motion.

"But, I mean, you're the *Neek*!"

"And you're another weird Terran," she muttered.

The man rubbed at his forehead. "Just...*wow!*"

Neek clenched her jaw. When the man said nothing more, she stood, but the Terran stood too and stepped in front of her. Yorden *wanted* to step in then, but Neek likely enjoyed a good bar fight as much as he did.

"Do we have a problem?" Neek asked, balling her fists.

The man held his hands up and shook his head. "No, no. Of course not. But you're *her.* In school, we learned that Neeks aren't even *allowed* to leave their world because you're all afraid you're going to miss the second coming of your god planet." He leaned back against the bar and seemed to puff his chest. "So, if your planet-thing does come, what does that mean for you? Religiously, I mean."

"It's not going to come, and if it does, I don't give a *titha* ass," she said acerbically. "If you want to debate theology, I can give you my uncle's personal comm line. It's not like I'm using it."

He took a step closer to her, his hands becoming more animated. Yorden stiffened. This was not boding well for his chances of Neek agreeing to his offer. "Yeah, but if it does exist, right—let's just say it does—and it comes, and you're here, do all the other Neeks go on the planet and zoom off to heaven or something and you're left here with the rest of the dregs? Does that keep you up at night?"

"Could we please stop talking about this?"

"Huh?" His eyes kept roaming, but not in a "let's go somewhere quiet" way. No, now he was going to drink in every last detail of her appearance and her accent, and if Neek didn't hit the guy soon, Yorden would.

"So, what's it like?" he asked in an excited whisper.

Neek wrinkled her nose. "What's what like? Talking with strange Terrans in bars?"

He laughed and then gestured at her torso. "This. You. Your exploratory mission of one. The involuntary Youth Journey, as it were."

That was too far. Yorden pushed his way to the bar.

"The *what*?"

The man's smile turned vaguely predatory. "I know you're an exile. Hell, the whole Charted Systems knows you're an exile. What's it like wandering the galaxy in search of meaning and handsome men willing to buy you drinks?"

"She'd have to find some, first." Yorden came up behind her suitor, snorted, and raised an eyebrow. He had to play this exactly right, or he'd be out of a pilot before she even looked at him. Not a rescue, but a well-timed intervention. Yorden was definitely not dashing enough to be a hero anyway. "You gamble, Neek?" he asked, nonchalant.

"Get lost, buddy." The blond man tried to push Yorden back, which was ridiculous. Yorden was twice his width, and a jazzercise butt only got you so far. The man nudged Yorden's hip thrice, each time progressively harder, until Yorden finally elbowed him so hard that the blond man crashed to the floor, wheezing.

Yorden held out his right hand to Neek, palm up. "I'm Yorden Kuebrich, Captain of *Mercy's Pledge*. You gamble?"

Neek blinked slowly and looked from the gasping man to the bar at large. No one was even looking at them, not even the bartender, which Neek appeared to have trouble processing.

"Well?"

"Didn't...didn't I see you on that Oorin station?"

Well, she was paying attention. Bonus for piloting, but hopefully he wasn't coming across as stalker-level creepy.

The man on the floor got his knees under him, and Yorden kicked them back out while he tried to figure out how best to play his hand. The yellow-haired man collapsed again. Neek took a step back.

Right. She needed space. He definitely didn't want her backed into a corner. He knew exactly what he'd do in such a situation, and they were far too similar to take that risk.

"Oorin Station? You mean Callis Spaceport?" Yorden asked, trying to keep his voice bland. "Yeah, I did see you there. You slimed me, then got thrown around by a Risalian asshat. Hard to forget. Anyway, cards? No one at my table cares how many fingers you have."

Neek shoved her hands back into her pockets and stared at Yorden, emotions playing across her face. He'd lose her in another minute unless she got a hook, which meant it was time to put an offer on the table.

"I need a pilot."

Neek's eyes became sharp, her jaw clenching. The blond man groaned on the floor, but Neek didn't even glance his way.

Yorden inclined his head toward his table. "I want to see how you do with something that isn't my ship first. Come sit." He pushed his way around a few patrons and back to the cheap plastic table. He didn't look back to make sure Neek followed, but he was relieved when she came up next to him.

"But I don't gamble," Neek said incredulously as she eyed the other card players. "I'm just a pilot."

"And we're just tramp captains," Yorden rebutted. He pulled a scarred plastic chair out for her and pointed at it. She didn't sit immediately, which was understandable, so Yorden gave her a moment to take in the crowd. One of the Terrans, the paler of the two, was missing both eyes.

The other had his hair shaved into two purple circles on either side of his head and had clearly had his nose broken one too many times. The Minoran was heavily tattooed and missing both his tail and back left leg. They were all old like Yorden—well past their prime—but carried enough institutional memory that they could have been museums on their own.

"Sit," Yorden demanded, taking the pageantry up a notch. Big hands or not, if she couldn't even be goaded into defiance, she wasn't going to be a good fit for the *Pledge*.

When Neek hesitated, he made a grand gesture of sweeping off the seat. "Little Journey youth. You want to fly, then you have to play. Sit."

Neek's hands came out of her pockets, trailing *stuk*. "Andal screw you," she snarled in Common. "I don't need this job." She turned and tried to push around various unwashed beings to the door, leaving a clear and wet trail of *stuk* in her wake.

Yorden grinned.

"I think you'll find 'go fuck yourself' more appropriate!" he yelled back smugly. "And you do want a job, because Oorin dredgers are dull as fuck, and I doubt you left your homeworld to babysit an intra-system diamond transport."

"I got *exiled*." Neek stalked back to him, her fists balled, her *stuk* now flaking white.

One of the Terrans at the table chuckled.

Neek spat on the ground. "Why would I choose you? I don't even *know* you."

Yorden met the raw emotion with the best thing he could offer: facts. "Because you're too thin and the Risalians don't care enough about Neek physiology to see that you're not meeting your calorie counts. Because you're depressed and no amount of *stuk* can hide the scars on your arms. Because you belong here. Well, not *here* here, but out in the broader Charted Systems. Where there's opportunity. And ships. And people who don't give a fuck about Ardulum." His voice lowered. "I'd have thought that was obvious."

"How about I punch you in that *bilaris* fly nest on your face? And when you swing back, you'll get arrested, but I'll only get a lecture, and we'll see how sanctimonious you feel as you're hauled out of here by Risalian sheriffs."

Yorden's stomach flipped to the sound of the other captains laughing. That was good steel she was showing, but not quite the right kind. "Journey youth" was a safety net she couldn't keep using if she signed with him. Yorden decided to prod a bit deeper. "Playing the Journey youth victim card? Maybe you do belong in this bar, then."

"I *belong* back on Neek!"

"Yeah? So, why are you here?" He pointed to her seat and then slapped two red bioplastic cards in front of her. The Minoran put a tall glass of clear liquid in front of them. "You think you're going to get back to your planet working mineral transport? You think you won't slowly starve to death on that dredger with Oorin food that your body can barely digest? Think following the rules and being a good little Journey youth who keeps her head down is going to keep the Risalians out of your business? You don't know a goddamned thing about the Systems, do you, Neek?"

Finally, she came for him directly. "I know tramp transport isn't a profession a parent would encourage. Are you even allowed to sign Journey youths, or is your ship such a waste of space that you can't afford anyone else?"

Yorden pointed a finger toward her. He didn't have to fake these emotions. Someone taking jabs at the *Pledge* hurt. "I'll tell you what I know, kid. I know the Risalians don't have enough cutters to spare to run their Neek andal to Risal. I know they hire *tramp* transports 'cause no one else wants to mess with your finicky, little shit trees. I'm in your planet's orbit half a dozen times a year, and Journey youths don't have to register on a manifest with their name or species. And I figure you—despite being a stuck-up, entitled teenager used to having the world listen to her every whine—would give just about anything to get back to a world where you're not simultaneously a nobody and the galaxy's biggest celebrity."

Neek didn't have any words. Well, Yorden supposed she had a lot of unproductive words, but he *had* her, and she knew it. He knew what exile meant for her. He knew who she was. Yorden was a betting man, and he would bet the *Mercy's Pledge* that there was a settee-shaped hole in Neek, and she'd give just about anything—would put up with just about anything—o get a glimpse of her homeworld again.

Still, he didn't want her defeated. He needed her defiant, and she wasn't quite there yet.

Neek sat.

"Rounds," the eyeless human said, tapping the table. "Put 'em out."

Neek glared at Yorden and then emptied her pockets. Two rounds, a small thimbleful of lint, and something pink and jiggly that looked a little too much like Spam got added to the center pot. Yorden cursed to himself. Either she was horrible with money, which he doubted, or the Oori weren't paying her shit.

Neek reached for the top card, fingers gummy with *stuk*. The thin bioplastic stuck instantly, and she flicked her wrist, trying to dislodge it. In doing so, she spread her hand as wide as she could, stretching all eight digits. Yorden grunted. The Minoran neighed. They didn't care how *many* fingers she had, sure, but her handspan was still pretty damn impressive.

Neek snarled and downed the drink in front of her. Yorden didn't even know what was in it. They'd already finished the Minoran pisco-like drink, and he hadn't touched his single malt yet. The whatever-it-was probably hit her fast given her practically concave stomach. Neek grimaced, coughed, and then retried to dislodge the card. The bioplastic held fast to her *stuk*.

"I don't even know the rules," she muttered.

"Hit or stay," the Minoran returned. "Pick one or the other."

"Stay." She said the word with a sneer, which Yorden definitely admired.

"You have a two and a five," Yorden said as the Minoran hit the other players. "Not a good call."

"I've got twenty-one!" the purple-haired Terran whooped and scooped the pot toward him. "Suckers!"

Neek swung her whole arm toward Yorden's midsection, flicking her wrist enough to send the wet card onto his chest, where it stuck. "I thought you wanted a pilot," she said through gritted teeth. "What am I doing here?"

Yorden ignored her question in favor of another jibe. She was too passive for a half-starved, exiled pilot being forced to gamble away her last rounds, and he needed to get them out of the bar, where they could talk without spectators. "I thought Neek were good with their hands, or were you exiled for being awkward?"

"Shut up!" Neek stood and pushed the deck across the table, the top few cards sliding off and onto the floor. Of course, another few stuck to her palm. She pulled them off with a squelching sound and a long string of clear mucus that she flung in Yorden's direction.

"There's a Journey youth lodge down the road. Nice warm bed, and they're probably playing Go Fish. More your speed?"

Neek screamed, grabbed the sandwich-shaped perf in front of Yorden, and stormed out of the bar, exiting through the emergency door to the back alley. After a few moments, Yorden followed, far enough behind that she hopefully wouldn't notice him. Small mammals skittered in the darkness, and the air smelled like urine and feces. He knew the alleys here well enough. They were all gross, stinking shitholes. Even if he lost sight of her for a few moments, there were few places she could go.

Except, she was clearly savvy enough to know she was being followed. From at least two alleyways over, Yorden heard her shout at him.

"I can find my own damn way to Neek! I don't need handouts from some fluffy Terran old enough to be my grandfather. So, damn you, damn Terrans, and damn Mars!"

Yorden followed the sound of her voice around a crumbling biometal wall to behind a discarded sofa. Mars' two oblong moons reflected enough light that he could see her silhouette among the piles of trash and the occasional patch of red soil.

Neek didn't turn to look at him. Instead, she attacked the perf—cramming a large corner into her mouth, seemingly oblivious to how dry and bland it tasted—and kicked the wall.

"Is there anywhere in the Charted Systems I can go where I won't be patronized like a teenager or gawked at like an endangered animal?" she asked, mouth full, although Yorden wasn't sure if she was asking him or the wall. He stayed silent.

A slow breeze kicked up a swirl of red dirt and tossed it down the alley. It brought a chill as well, and Neek shivered, took a deep breath, and leaned back against the wall. Her eyes closed.

Calm, unfortunately, wasn't where he needed her. A calm Neek would go right back to her dredger and slowly starve herself to death so she could avoid Journey youth hostels and beings who cared about how many fingers she had. Yorden knew depression, and he knew diaspora, and while Neek didn't need a savior, she sure as hell needed a friend. Preferably a friend with access to her homeworld.

And Yorden needed a pilot.

"It smells like shit out here. You're better off inside, even with that piss-haired suitor of yours."

Neek threw the mashed remains of the perf at Yorden's head. The food crumbled into his beard, bits drifting to the packed dirt below. He stayed still, forcing himself not to react.

"Would you just leave me *alone*?"

Yorden stared at her, one hand on the brick wall. He carefully schooled his tone to neutral. "I'd like to offer you a job, I think."

"Go fuck a *titha*!" she spat back. "I'm not here for your amusement."

"This would be a bad place for it," Yorden responded calmly. He shook out the crumbs from his beard. "You're a long way from 'badass with a blaster.' We could fix that though—the blaster part. I've got a bit of a collection. You'd be welcome to investigate it."

Neek kicked the wall again, sending up a plume of red dust, and snarled.

Yorden dropped all pretense. This was where he had wanted her—angry, her pride stripped away so she could see how much shit she was in. Not that she couldn't make it on her own—hell, he had, but his life would have been a shit-ton easier with another person who maybe halfway understood what it was like to live on the fringe of the Systems.

"Kid, listen. From the way that shirt hangs on your shoulders and the way you keep licking your lips, I'd say you were hungry. Oorin food printers aren't designed with bipeds in mind, so I'd say that you've been hungry for a while. Maybe you took that gig because you wanted a job— a reliable one, although maybe not a safe one—away from crowded bars and ogling eyes." He leaned against the wall but came no closer. "It would be better on the *Pledge*. I mean, not a *lot* better, but some. You wouldn't be starving anyway." He wasn't goading, and he wasn't baiting. He was a captain, and this was a job offer. A solid one. And Neek was finally in a place to really listen to it.

"I don't want anything from *you*," Neek barked. "I was handling that man just fine. My job is fine. I'm *fine*."

Yorden shrugged. "Then, by all means, go back inside. But I thought you were looking for a pilot job? I'm interested in finding a pilot with a wide handspan and a low tolerance for bullshit. You fit the bill perfectly. Interested?"

"No."

Yorden crossed his arms. "Really? My ship maneuvers a lot better than a dredger. Don't tell me that doesn't set your heart aflutter. A tramp is a long way from a dredger, and a very long way from a back alley on Mars."

Neek took a long time to respond. So long, in fact, that Yorden thought he might have misread the situation—pushed her too far. He mentally berated himself and tried to figure out how he could fix the situation, or at the very least not have the kid run off to a worse job than she already had. But, before he could open his mouth, Neek finally met his eyes, and Yorden saw hope there for the first time.

"Why are you asking *me*?" she asked tightly.

Yorden almost shrugged, but then thought better of it. "I need a pilot, and I think we have a decent chance of not killing each other inside tight quarters. Also, I—" He choked on the next words. "I maybe could use someone to talk shit to on long hauls. The *Pledge* isn't much for conversation."

"I'm not at all personable," Neek responded.

"That isn't part of the job description."

Neek rubbed at her nose, and Yorden watched those little sparks of hope turn into a blaze. "I like precision flying. No guesswork. Charts, maps, appropriate use of fuel with the occasional dynamic display to test turn radii. And I don't like to be told how to do my job."

"Not many do. You'll have your own quarters and your own code for the food printer and the comm. Pay is standard monthly and based upon a percentage of the profits. The percentage is negotiable."

"If I have my own quarters and the printer is free, I don't care how much you pay, but it better be in diamond rounds," Neek shot back.

"The *Mercy's Pledge* only deals with Charted Systems standard currency and Charted Systems hauls. I don't do rules. I don't do laws. I move what I want to move, when I want to move it. But"—he raised an eyebrow—"I'm not interested in hiring runaways. I need a great pilot that won't ditch me the first time we get fired upon or have a lean month. Is that you? Or are you too caught up in this martyred urchin thing to be useful?"

That last jab was useless, and Yorden regretted it the moment it left his mouth.

"I was exiled," she spat and pulled at her tattered shirt. "I'm a fine pilot. You can ask my current captain for a reference if you want. But this"—she kicked at the red soil—"being here...none of this was by choice."

Yorden grunted in agreement because none of them were here by choice, just circumstance. No one came to a stinking bar on Mars because they wanted to. They were all inexorably wrapped in this whole "perfect peace" bullshit the Risalians were peddling.

"Time to make a choice, then. Fuck the Risalians. Do things your way. Our way. See the galaxy through your own eyes." He lowered his voice, trying to be comforting. "See your planet, Neek."

Neek sank to her knees into the red dirt, squelching into something wet. Yorden saw tears glisten in her eyes, and his stomach sank.

"I'm not going to cry," Neek hissed to herself, but Yorden heard her anyway. "There's no reason to cry. I didn't really like it there. It's just a planet."

The tears came. They skirted around her cheeks, diverted by *stuk* trails as she tried to wipe her face clean. Yorden heard her stomach rumble. "How ridiculous is it to get on a ship with a man I barely know to live out the palest version of my dream, to torment myself with a planet I can see but never again touch?"

"Better than kneeling in someone else's vomit in an alley?" Yorden asked softly. "It's safer for sure than working in mineral transport, wearing out the tendons in your hands, and spending shore leave begging for scraps in bars and spaceports. In another year, you won't qualify as a Journey youth anymore. What then? You'll be a dishwasher, maybe, in some restaurant, or have some equally lonely, soul-destroying job. You could be *flying*."

Neek's eyes narrowed. "Screw Ardulum. I'm not that pathetic." She stood, pulling her knees from the puddle with a slurping sound. She wiped her face again, further smearing her tears and *stuk*, and set her jaw.

And there it was. There *she* was—a pilot who was looking more and more like a decent person to befriend, too. Bitterness loved company, especially on a derelict tramp. Yorden took three steps toward her, ignoring the filth that streamed around and over his bare feet. He held out one mammoth hand—not for her to take, but rather as a gesture of friendliness. An invitation. "C'mon, kid. You don't belong here."

An aborted chuckle bubbled from Neek's throat. Yorden chuckled as well. He couldn't help it. Together, they walked out of the alley, onto the main road of dusty, red bricks, and toward the glistening field of spaceships on the city's perimeter. Surprising warmth sparked across Yorden's chest as he led her past cruisers, skiffs, dredgers, miners, and barges to his old Buran shuttle.

The nose of the shuttle sagged precariously close to the ground, the armor plating was unevenly riveted, and its dorsal fins stuck out at weird angles; he still hadn't even finished resecuring the antique laser turret to the hull. It was a cracked, dented, bent, off-white, antique monstrosity, but when Neek followed Yorden inside and saw the cockpit console with its old steering yoke *and* computer interface, she only smiled. She saw the same thing he did. The potential. The freedom.

Without invitation, Neek sat in the pilot's leather chair. The cushioning gave an audible sigh as her rear sank below the chair's rim. Yorden knew how that seat felt. Worn in. Old. Comfortable. Like it knew you. She looked over at him, and Yorden nodded solemnly because years of Terran conditioning wouldn't let him show he was as excited about this as she was.

"The *Pledge* gets a vote in this too. So far, you're passing."

Neek snorted in a nearly perfect imitation of him, splayed her left hand across the console, hooking her thumb and first two fingers around the yoke, and tapped on the computer with her remaining digits. Her *stuk* smeared across the controls. She flicked off the safeties, powered the thrusters, and edged the nose of the ship up, angling toward the atmosphere. Toward Neek, Yorden surmised. He understood completely.

"Permission to launch, Captain?" Neek asked, breathless.

"You got a name, kid? Other than that common name your people love to give yourselves?"

Neek shook her head, keeping her eyes fixed on the sky. "Just Neek," she murmured. "Just a Neek."

"All right then, Neek. How about you take us through the Terran Wormhole and head toward Baltec, in the Minoran System. There's a haul I need to pick up there." When that felt too callous for the moment, he added, "Glad to have you."

Neek's hands shook, but only just. "I can call my former captain from here and let them know I'm not coming back, but don't you need to file a petition with the Youth Journey offices for me to change my contract?"

Yorden gave her a bland look. "Do I look like I care about Risalian rules? Are you my pilot, or aren't you?"

Neek closed her eyes and shook her head. A smile twitched at the corners of her mouth. "No, Captain. I'm all yours. I'm a pilot."

"Then, take us to Baltec, Neek."

Joy burst across her face, and Yorden felt it too—soaring through his chest and into a smile as wide as the horizon. Neek sent power to the thrusters and brought *Mercy's Pledge* up, slowly at first, above the other ships, above the city. Building speed, it broke the bonds of the atmosphere and, finally, powered into space itself.

Palace Politics

Second Month of Arath, 16_15

"You're not supposed to be in the kitchens, Eki. You know that."

Ekimet shoved the remainder of a cinnamon-spiced andal twig into zir pocket and put zir hands on top of the counter. Zie wasn't wearing a shirt but refused to blush. It was the kitchen and the middle of the night. Shirts were optional. "I got lost," zie blurted out.

Savath appeared at the doorway to the kitchens and frowned. "I doubt that very much."

Ekimet's mind raced to find another plausible excuse. Zie was too tired for a lecture, and Savath's serious expression was already making zir feel like an andal stump was pushing against zir chest. "Yeah, well, you're the one who showed me how to sneak down here in the first place. Technically, this is your fault."

Savath held out zir hand, the sleeve of zir long, silver robe pooling onto the counter. "That was because it was your first night, and you needed something to distract you. Come on back. I know it's a hard transition from living at home to living in the Eld Palace's gatoi quarters, but it's been almost three years. We're second *don* now—both of us. You have to stop these nighttime wanderings."

Ekimet pushed Savath's hand away. "So, why are you up?"

Savath rolled zir eyes. "Because I'm responsible for you, *titha* head. If you get in trouble, it's my fault."

"Oh. Right." Ekimet looked at the grain of the countertop, wishing zie could fall into the earlywood and disappear. Zie had wanted a snack, but it wasn't worth Savath getting yelled at by the Eld—especially since they would undoubtedly revoke Savath's day pass into town. And if Savath didn't get to leave the palace, then neither did Ekimet. Mentors like Savath only got a pass every other month. If Ekimet or Savath got caught tonight, then it would be some very depressing next few months.

"I'm sorry, Savath. I wasn't thinking."

Savath put a hand on Ekimet's shoulder. "Lonely, still?"

Ekimet snorted.

"You know," Savath said, moving away and leaning on the countertop, "it's okay to be lonely, but you don't have to be lonely alone. There are over one hundred of us here from all over Ardulum. Plus, you have me. You could have just knocked on my door."

Ekimet ignored the warm joviality of Savath's words. Zie had been here a year longer than Ekimet. Zie had probably forgotten what it was like to run down a hill without someone screaming at you to be careful, forgotten what it was like to skin and clean a *titha* without someone taking the knife from your hands because one slip and you could cut yourself and—no. No, they couldn't have that. Couldn't risk getting their precious gatois injured. No injuries. No risks. No life. Ekimet was sick of it all, and even more sick of the fact that no one seemed to miss their former lives except zir.

Besides, Savath had plenty of other friends.

"No one ever tells you what it's going to be like after your metamorphosis," Ekimet whispered. "Not for us, anyway. Doesn't that ever bother you?"

"It's considered an honor to be chosen to be schooled here. Not every gatoi gets the opportunity. Some are asked to join families immediately. Some have Talents that are needed so badly that they start working directly. But some, like us, get to have a real education." Savath slid closer to Ekimet and wrapped long fingers around Ekimet's hand. Savath's touch usually comforted, but tonight, Ekimet felt too wound up. A dream had woken zir, but zie couldn't remember the specifics, just something about talking trees. Silly, of course, because andal couldn't talk in the typical sense, but it had left Ekimet with an uneasy feeling zie couldn't shake.

"Yeah? You lost your apprenticeship on New Ubtarot because of this 'opportunity.' The Eld canceled all our second-*don* apprenticeships. How can you be okay with that?"

"It *is* an opportunity, just a different one," Savath chided. "Come on. Let me take you back to your room."

"It'd only be an opportunity if I was given a choice!" Ekimet pulled zir hand from Savath's and stepped back, hitting the cooling unit. "You can pretend to not be upset about the apprenticeships being taken away, but I refuse to just be happy stewing in one place. Savath, I want to go home." Zie pointed to the hexagons on zir left shoulder. "I'm a Hearth Talent, but even here they won't let me into the kitchen, or the machine shop, or the livestock fields. All we do is read. I can already speak four languages. When am I going to get to *do* something?"

Savath dropped zir arms to zir sides, studying Ekimet intently. Ekimet tried not to fidget under zir gaze, especially when zir eyes moved from zir Talent markings to Ekimet's cropped, dark-auburn hair. Gatois usually had long hair, but Ekimet had been ready to run last week, too, and Savath had offered the haircut as a rebellion.

It hadn't been enough.

"I'm leaving," Ekimet said, zir voice low. "I want to file for dismissal from the program."

Savath bit zir lower lip before pulling over two hardwood chairs and motioning for Ekimet to sit. "Have any of that cinnamon andal left to share?" zie asked. "Last meal with your mentor? Friend?"

A smile quirked at the corners of Ekimet's mouth. Savath had been there for every meltdown, every triumph, every late-night wandering. They came from the same region, so Ekimet had at first assumed zir patience with zir was out of misplaced solidarity, but over the years, Savath had become someone more like a friend. Also, zie apparently wasn't going to turn Ekimet in for swiping andal, so it was best to share the bounty.

Ekimet unearthed the small twig from zir pocket, broke it in half, and handed the unchewed end to Savath. Their fingers brushed, but this time, the contact made Ekimet jump. Just a little.

Savath had been assigned Ekimet's mentor when zie had presented zirself at the Eld Palace in zir seventeenth year of life, as was customary for gatois. Male and female first *dons* got to have their full twenty years at home. Gatois only got seventeen, which had always seemed like an unfair amount of time. Savath was friendly and warm, much like all the gatois in their palatial "holding pens," but every so often, Ekimet saw...a glimpse of someone else. Maybe it was a shadow of who Savath had been in zir first *don*. Maybe it was a glimmer of zir third *don* to come. Or, maybe it was the way Savath listened when Ekimet spoke, zir eye contact unrelenting, as if Ekimet were the only person that mattered on all of Ardulum. They weren't the same type of gatoi—Savath was i-type intersex, born with gatoi-specific genitals, while Ekimet had been born presenting male and had chosen to transition to gatoi later—and sometimes that mattered. Sometimes, but not to Ekimet.

Whatever it was, that other Savath was the reason Ekimet was still here, in the palace kitchens, instead of back in zir parents' apartment in the crowded, noisy city of Ellthuy, the capital city of Ardulum's only equatorial continent.

Savath's eyes were staring now, digging into Ekimet while they both ate. "It really is delicious," Savath said as zie finished the twig and licked zir fingers clean. Still, zir eyes stayed on Ekimet's.

"We're both fugitives," Ekimet whispered conspiratorially. "Maybe they'll lock us up in a dungeon. That'd at least be something new."

Savath laughed. "Well, then. If dungeons are already on the table, I say we go for it." Zie pointed to the cooling unit. "I think this batch is for the Eld's party tomorrow. They probably wouldn't miss one more, right?"

Ekimet grinned. "Do we care?"

To Ekimet's delight, Savath hopped from the chair and made an exaggerated show of tiptoeing to the unit, easing open the door, gently dragging a twig from the center of the stack, and then putting the door back into place. "Spoils of war," zie said, breaking off half and handing it to Ekimet. "You're going to get me in so much trouble."

Ekimet put the end of the twig in zir mouth and sucked at the seasoned sap. "Bet you've never been in trouble before, have you? Not in the years I've been here, and not before, either."

Savath's gaze dropped unexpectedly to the counter, zir expression distant. Ekimet put the andal down, instantly regretting zir words. "Sorry, Savath. Did I say something wrong?"

Savath shook zir head, and when zie looked back up, Savath was smiling, zir melancholy vanished. Ekimet once again felt like the center of zir world. The fragmented andal dreams, the anger over the rescinded apprenticeships, the loneliness…it all slipped from Ekimet's mind.

"What did you like to do before you came here? What were your dreams?" Savath asked. They'd never really talked about the "before," because being in the palace was all about their *futures*, but the question seemed far from invasive.

"I studied diplomacy, mostly," Ekimet answered, sitting back in zir chair. If zir stomach had been fluttering moments ago, then it had at least settled. "I'd heard that it's one of the best ways to get out of the palace early if you don't want to head right for family life. Well, I studied flares a lot, too, at my grandmother's insistence, but I don't think there's a future in that. But we haven't been in the Alliance—well, the center of it—for that long, and the Keft thing was a disaster. Diplomats must be in high demand."

"Mm, I agree. That's why they picked me to mentor you. I like the same stuff. Speaking of which, guess who finally got permission to work in the foundry?"

Ekimet sprang to zir feet. "Wait, you get to work in the foundry?!"

Savath's eyes lit up as zie stuck out zir tongue. "Jealous?"

Ekimet smacked zir on the shoulder. "Eternally."

"If you wanted to stay, I'm sure I could speak to the Eld and see if you could get in too."

Ekimet let zir head fall to one side as zie frowned. "You've resorted to bribery? Why? Even with the foundry, you'd still end up chasing me around this place, trying to get me to, I don't know, wear silver robes and braid my hair."

Savath tugged Ekimet back down to the chair and leaned in toward zir ear. "I'm not hearing a no. Besides, I thought you liked it when I braided your hair."

Ekimet's heart thumped against zir ribs. Home was great, and far less suffocating, but zir family didn't have anything close to a blacksmith setup. That *was* one of the reasons Ekimet had first allowed zirself to be talked into being schooled at the palace. There were opportunities here that zie would never get anywhere else. Still...

"Savath, I...I'd need something else. Plus, they'd never just let me walk in and—"

Ekimet's words stuttered to a stop as zie felt hands on zir shoulders. Between one moment and the next, there were lips on zir lips. Savath's lips. Kissing Ekimet. Zie had no idea how to respond, and Savath didn't seem to know how to proceed, so they held the position for several heartbeats. Savath's breath tasted like cinnamon. The smell filled Ekimet's nose and sinuses and made zir throat feel tight. Zie tried to swallow, tried to think, but the only two thoughts zie could manage was that Savath's lips were really smooth and that this was a lot different than the greeting kiss gatois normally used with each other. Ekimet liked it a lot more, and it made zir insides feel soft like springwood.

Savath pulled back, finally, zir face lightly flushed, zir breath ragged.

"You should have asked," Ekimet said as zie, too, struggled for breath.

"We never ask to kiss," Savath returned. "We're gatois."

Ekimet touched zir lips with two fingers. "That wasn't a gatoi kiss."

"Do you want to end up assigned to a couple?" Savath suddenly demanded, zir fingers tightening on Ekimet's shoulders. Zir words cut at Ekimet. What sort of conversation was this, anyway? First admonishment, then kissing—*kissing*—and then yelling? How was zie supposed to react? What was going on with Savath? Was this that other Savath Ekimet had only had glimpses of these past years?

"No," Ekimet answered, as evenly as zie could. "I don't want another cage. I want a job, and I want it away from Eld influence." Zie took Savath's hands from zir shoulders and gripped them. *I can break protocol, too,* zie said, creating a mental connection. *Not everyone is afraid to use telepathy. What do you want? Why are you here in the kitchens with me?*

Savath stared at Ekimet for a long moment before responding. *I want a lot of things I'm not allowed to have. You're not the only one who can't sleep at night.*

Ekimet considered the words, tossing various bizarre explanations aside, but not coming up with any rational ones.

Is one of those things me?

It seemed like a really silly question. It wasn't as if sex was some taboo subject in the palace, and no one expected the palace gatois to be celibate while in training, but they weren't supposed to be kissing *each other*. Still, Ekimet couldn't deny that the notion lit a fire in zir insides that began to spread outward, reaching zir fingertips and leaving a trembling in its wake.

I've not done much, but if you wanted to, we could, Ekimet added. *Do you want to go back to your room? Is that what you want?*

A smile ghosted across Savath's face. "I do—especially with you—but that's not the point."

Ekimet crossed zir arms. "Then, what is the point? You just kissed me, Savath, and we're both *sweating* because of it. Is this another rebellion to keep me here? Another haircut?" zie scoffed. "Little acts of treason aren't enough."

Savath's eyes flicked from Ekimet to the floor and back again. "It was silly," zie mumbled. "I'm sorry, Ekimet."

I didn't say I didn't like it, Ekimet admitted after a moment.

Although Savath's head was still lowered, Ekimet could see mischief hop back into Savath's eyes. "We could do more," Savath whispered. "The bedroom, the foundry, the kitchens. You let this place be a coffin and it becomes one. We don't get to make choices here, but a few extra activities to keep us happy, to keep us 'under control'? No one would mind."

Except, if that were true, why bother having rules at all? Ekimet didn't buy it. The gatoi training program at the palace was notoriously restrictive. You got the best jobs available when you got out, but it was at the expense of your entire second *don*. It was not a program one went into lightly, and flippant behavior was *not* tolerated.

"If no one cares, why did you follow me to the kitchen?" Ekimet asked.

Savath put a hand on Ekimet's knee—tentatively. Ekimet smiled and covered it with zir own. "Because I've never seen a gatoi here break a rule. I did, once, my first year. I'd never seen the Eld so mad."

Ekimet leaned in. "What did you do?"

Savath smiled and tapped a finger to zir lips. "What started as a greeting lingered a little too long. By accident, that time. I didn't realize how different it would be, kissing another gatoi. The world suddenly made sense."

Ekimet's insides twisted. Gatois didn't make families with other gatois. Ekimet wasn't even sure two gatois could produce children on their own. They were a spice, not a primary ingredient. Zie could easily imagine how the other student had reacted. How the Eld had reacted.

"Did you love zir?" Ekimet asked.

"Oh, no." Savath shook zir head and chortled. "It was an experience, and one I didn't bother replicating."

Ekimet raised an eyebrow. "Until now. The cinnamon go to your head?"

"I think we're a lot alike."

That made Ekimet pause. Were they? Or, was this just late-night euphoria brought on by shared secrets and petty theft? And if Ekimet stayed, would there be more lips and wandering hands and late-night strolls to beds in unoccupied rooms?

Ekimet felt lightheaded, but that was probably because zie hadn't taken a breath in a long time. Zie inhaled heavily, letting the cool night air clear zir head.

"We could get kicked out for what you're suggesting."

"You want to leave anyway."

Ekimet nodded. "Point. But you want to stay."

Savath squeezed Ekimet's knee, sending warmth flooding between Ekimet's legs. "We won't be kicked out, Eki."

"And you know this how?"

"Because the Eld are shopping."

"For not mateable gatoi?" If Savath was going to be willfully obtuse, then Ekimet would pry answers from Savath zirself. Zie moved zir hand onto Savath's thigh and slid it up to zir hip. Savath's breath caught. Ekimet's heart pounded.

"Are we trying to see how tight those boundaries are?" Ekimet whispered.

"Some...something like that." Savath scooted closer, forcing Ekimet's hand to slide inward. "They have some secret—the Eld—and I want it. There hasn't been a gatoi eld in four years. That's why the Eld keep us so penned up now. That's why we're not getting regular assignments until we're third *don*."

That surprised Ekimet enough that zie dropped zir hand away. Savath let out a long sigh, but Ekimet barely registered it. "They're keeping us penned in case we manifest another Talent in our third *don*? You think one of us will be the new gatoi eld? From our cohort?"

Savath rubbed zir red cheeks. "I think that's the elds' plan, yes."

Ekimet looked incredulously at Savath. "But it's not going to be either of us, surely! Look! I'm stealing desserts, and you're kissing me in the kitchen. I'm an entire decade away from my third *don*, and you've only been here a year longer than me. There are thirteen gatoi moving into third *don* next *month*. Why would Ardulum go nine or ten years without the full triarchy just to elevate Ardulans who don't even want to be here?"

Savath didn't seem to hear zir at all. "Do you have weird dreams, Eki?"

"Weirder than you're acting now? You know I do. We've talked about them. It's why I don't sleep well. You have them, too."

Savath nodded. "You know that no one else does?"

Ekimet brushed zir hand across the countertop. "I don't believe that. Everyone gets weird dreams sometimes." Zie stood, the last of the heat fading from zir face, zir heartbeat returning to its usual pitter-patter. Zie rotated one ankle and then the other, trying to get the pinpricks of inactivity to go away. "This is ridiculous. You want to press Eld buttons, or even just"—zie pointed in the direction of the gatoi apartments—"have some private discussions, then okay. But the best we can both hope for is an off-world assignment where they let us cut our own vegetables. I have no idea what you're trying to imply right now. I think we should go back to bed."

Ekimet expected a retort, or an abrupt change in conversation, but Savath just stared at zir, brown eyes unblinking.

"Argh! Do you want to go walking to the ship pads, then?" Ekimet tried. Getting out of the kitchens, away from

Savath's stare, seemed really important all of a sudden. "Some Mmnnuggls are visiting. Their ships are pretty neat."

"Be my friend, Ekimet."

Savath didn't ask it like a question, which was probably for the best because they weren't first *dons* and it would have been a juvenile question even at that age.

"I *am* your friend." Ekimet pulled Savath to zir feet and dragged zir out the back door of the kitchens and into the small andal garden. Zie purposefully did not look back at Savath's face. "Let's go look at ships."

"I was thinking of a different kind of friendship."

Ekimet stopped and spun around. Zie was tired of the meandering, obfuscated conversation. Savath needed to get to the point. "Savath, if you want to be lovers—"

"No." Savath released Ekimet's hand and pulled at one of the andal saplings, curving it down until the apical shoot was right at their noses. "This isn't about that. I mean, it is, partially, but it's about... I don't think Ardulum is supposed to be like this, Ekimet."

Ekimet looked around at the thin saplings covered in dimly lit, green leaves, at the four moons overhead, and the rise of purple-black pods just beyond. Savath let the andal go, and it sprang back into place, its leaves scratching against one another.

"What else would it be like?" Ekimet asked. "This is how Ardulum is."

Savath shook zir head. "I don't think it has to be."

"You think us making out is going to change our planet? Are you drunk?"

Savath winked at zir. A smirk crept up at the corner of zir mouth. Warmth came back to Ekimet's face. "Come on. One more year. Stay here with me. I'll get you into the foundry. I'll get you a job with the cooks. I'll even give you my day passes. Just *stay*."

"Wherever you got the fermented andal you are clearly on, I want some. Also, why? Why shouldn't I just get on one of the Mmnnuggl ships and let them fly me off

Ardulum and out of this system?" Ekimet's chest felt tight, almost like they were having a real, productive argument, instead of this inane *whatever*. Zie wanted to push Savath, or kiss zir, or just turn and run as far as zie could from the palace before the Eld found zir and brought zir back. "Savath, we're just *waiting* here. It's stupid."

Savath took zir hands. They faced each other, their noses centimeters apart. Ekimet could smell Savath's breath, could feel the heat coming from zir body. Zie swallowed against zir tightening throat, trying to match the intensity with which Savath's eyes bored into zirs.

"Ardulum is going to change, Ekimet." Savath's voice trembled. "I see it in my dreams."

"Maybe you're eating too much of that fermented andal."

Savath pushed into Ekimet's body, melding their hips together, bringing zir mouth way too close to Ekimet's ear. Ekimet felt dizzy. Drunk. Almost dangerous, like Savath was telepathically sharing zir delusion.

"We're a part of that change," Savath breathed.

"We're just gatoi," Ekimet said, but zie didn't back away. Stepping back would be a torture zie couldn't endure. Wherever this conversation was headed, Ekimet no longer cared. All that mattered was being here, close to Savath.

"Stay, and I promise I will get you a real assignment, not an apprenticeship, before your third *don*. Stay, and I promise I will tell you every Eld secret I know, every andal whisper I hear. Stay, and help me force these Eld to look at us as more than pretty attendants. You and I are not *just* gatoi."

They could melt together into the same person. Ekimet was sure of it. The evening was chilly, but the cold breeze was powerless against the warmth of Savath's skin on zirs. "What are we?" Ekimet asked. Zie cared, suddenly, about the answer.

Savath giggled, zir torso pushing into Ekimet's. Zie couldn't help but join in, and a moment later, they were laughing and hugging. Savath's mouth found Ekimet's again, briefly, before Ekimet pulled them apart.

"Help me?" Savath entreated. "Stay."

What are we? Ekimet asked again. *I'll stay for you, but Savath, what is this all about?*

I don't know, Savath responded. *But we don't have a gatoi eld, and there's got to be a reason for that.*

Ekimet raised an eyebrow. *So, we're going to...what? Break apart this palace and get some answers?*

Savath grinned, and for a moment, the way the moonlight hit zir silver robes made them look near gold. Ekimet shivered.

You in?

Ekimet nodded, took Savath's hand, and leaned into the taller gatoi. This wasn't at all how zie had thought zie would spend zir second *don*, but being this close to Savath settled the faint rustling in Ekimet's head that often came after a night of bad dreams. Maybe the Eld *were* plotting something. Maybe Savath was just bored. Ekimet didn't care. It was just really nice to have a...a friend. Or whatever.

Yes, I'm in. And I suggest we start with the rest of the cinnamon andal because raiding the library or whatever you have in mind will be a lot more fun on a full stomach.

Youth Journey

2059 CE

"Nicholas St. John?"

"Present!" Nicholas jumped up from the plastic bench that circled the inside of the Journey office on Corieus, the third planet of the Minoran System. Squeezed into the room with him were some seventy fresh-faced Terran youths, all of whom had arrived that day for placement.

Nicholas stumbled, accidentally stepping on the feet of the larger boy next to him. The boy frowned at him, but Nicholas wrinkled his nose and didn't even try to fight his smile. He was *here.* He was doing it, really going on Journey! He was eighteen—legally an adult—and he was off his planet, outside his solar system, and he was going to talk to aliens! He was going to *work* for aliens!

Earth had joined the Charted Systems back in 2020, but Youth Journey hadn't been officialized until 2025, so his parents had never gotten a chance to go. Nicholas had spent the past few years watching friends and family leave Earth. They had adventures and otherworldly experiences and came home two years later as completely different people, full of stories and languages and ideas. There were no storybook adventures anymore—not like the kind he'd read as a kid that had pirates or musketeers or epic space battles—because the Systems were at peace, but Youth Journey was better because it was *his* journey. *His* adventure.

Finally, it was time for Nicholas to be an adult.

"St. John! You listening?"

Nicholas straightened his back and nodded. The large being that clopped toward him was a quadruped native to the Minoran System with the elongated torso and gray hair common to those from Corieus. He looked like a centaur, or maybe closer to if a centaur and a horse had offspring. Was that a thing? The anatomy probably lined up right, but there was a lot more torso on a centaur. So, if the horse was a female and had to carry the baby...

"St. John!" The Minoran stomped his back hoof.

"Sorry, sir!" Nicholas bit his lower lip and clasped his hands behind his back. "I was just thinking about biology."

"I'm sure. You've got an interview. Room eighteen. Law firm on Risal, per your mother's written request." The Minoran tossed a rolled-up biofilm at Nicholas, which he caught, hastily unrolled, and read.

Law Offices of Jak, Run, and Wer. Specializing in historic accounting law, religious disputes, and space travel violations. Seeking full-time Journey youth for filing, courier work, note taking, and research. No gender preference. All-species lavatories available. Paid.

Nicholas let out a heavy sigh. "Is there anything else?"

The Minoran twitched an ear. "There are plenty of other options, but *this* is what your mother asked for, and you signed up for it back on Earth. Little late to be changing your mind now, kid. Go do the interview. You can always turn them down."

The Minoran turned to the woman who had been sitting next to Nicholas, a Terran with black hair that was long on one side and shaved on the other. She wore the same green coveralls Nicholas did, with the word *YOUTH* embroidered on the right side. They'd been chatting only moments ago about their plans. Her name was Watchara, Nicholas remembered. Her skin was a warm, tawny brown, and she had soft features and wide eyes. Definitely pretty. He'd never tell her that.

"Watchara Eka, you have an interview with a tramp transport. Room seventeen. Go, both of you. I've got seventy more Terrans to get through, and you're wasting their time."

Watchara stood, but Nicholas barely paid attention as she moved toward the numbered offices. *Law.* It made his mouth feel dry. It made his lip curl. He was good at law, but it just didn't seem very…something. Very romantic? Very…adventurous? Besides, law wasn't the only thing he was good at. He knew about cellulose tech, too, and microbiology, and all the weird physics that went on with space travel, but his mom wanted him tucked away. Probably requested Risal in the hopes that he wouldn't come home with a hundred new curse words in alien languages like his sister, Hayley, or with a taste for live insects like his cousin.

"You coming?"

"Huh?"

Watchara had doubled back for him, hands on her narrow hips, wrinkling the coveralls. She had calluses on her knuckles. Nicholas looked at his own hands. The skin was more of an umber brown, but it was smooth and unblemished. No wonder she got tramp transport and he got law. His hands were wide and his fingers long, but they were made for books, not ships. Besides, tramp transport probably didn't pay well. Anything on Risal was sure to come with a solid paycheck.

Watchara's fingers snapped in front of his face. Nicholas blinked. "Sorry. I daydream. I'm ready."

"Good, because you're going to make us late. Not a good first impression, you know?" She grabbed Nicholas by the shoulder and hauled him through the bioplastic double doors and into the hall of offices. They'd been in the round receiving room of the Youth Journey Regional Office for close to two hours, but Nicholas had seen nothing except said room and the biped bathroom. All the surfaces had looked sterile and beige, with the Youth Journey logo painted in green across any space long enough to house it. He hadn't gotten to see *any* aliens, either, since the shuttle he'd been on had gone straight from Earth to Corieus. Well, any aliens except the grumpy Minoran.

Hopefully, that was about to change. Thus far, Youth Journey wasn't really living up to its potential, which meant Nicholas wasn't either.

It wasn't until the doors to the receiving room closed—blocking out the sounds of chattering Terrans—that Watchara released him. She slowed her pace, and Nicholas matched it as he tried to discern the numbering system on the doors.

"So, your interview sounds...fun." Watchara giggled, but the humor didn't reach her eyes.

"I guess." Nicholas tried to put some enthusiasm into the words but couldn't find any. "Where are you from? United States? I'm from Minnesota. It's upper Midwest."

Watchara turned to look at him. "Yeah, Atlanta, Georgia. Most of the people on our transport were from North America. But, like, you really want to do law? There's, like, nothing to law about anymore. You'll be up to your elbows in dusty paper books, I bet, if Risalians even have books. Dream bigger, friend. Tramp transport at least takes you places."

Nicholas shoved his hands into his pockets and frowned. "Maybe, but I'm a lot less likely to get space lice with law. *Tramp* transport? Did you request that?"

Watchara shrugged. They hit the first L-junction, where the doors began to have numbers in Common instead of one of the Minoran languages. Watchara squinted at the sloppy yellow paint. "Naw, just took the first thing that came." She pointed at the diagonal twenty-two on the first door to their right. "I don't think that was painted by someone with opposable thumbs."

"Does that matter? Is that a thing out in space, whether or not someone has thumbs? Is it like the not wearing shoes thing?"

She shrugged again. "Maybe. I dunno." She brightened. "Hey, want to come with me on the tramp? I mean, I'm eighteen, same as you. I haven't seen anything worth seeing, but it'd still be nice to spend Journey with someone anatomically compatible. You know?"

Nicholas tugged at the collar of his coveralls. It was a lot hotter in this hallway than it had been a minute ago. "Not really."

"No?" She stopped walking and put her hands on her hips. "That's fine, but, like, what *do* you want? Not law, apparently, or your enthusiasm slider maxes at, like, two. Not sex, which is totally your prerogative, but there has to be *something*. What are your scores?"

"Scores?" Nicholas's brow wrinkled. "On what?"

"Your *exit* scores. Come on."

Nicholas giggled nervously. "Oh, right. I got honors on my bio-composites and history of cellulose exams. Standard one ranking on everything else."

"Huh. I got honors on Common and interstellar mathematics. Couple of twos though on things like history, especially cellulose history. That stuff is dry. 'Course, you're going into law, so you probably love it." Watchara winked at him.

"But I don't, I mean, love it." Nicholas scrambled for the right words. How did one respond to a wink? Another wink? A bow? He wasn't any good at this flirting stuff. Still, she was being friendly, and Nicholas wasn't about to be rude. "I just...want to be in space, you know? In, like, a cutter or a skiff, or one of those other zippy ships." He mimed making a sharp turn with a round steering wheel. "Juking, dodging asteroids, and stuff. Learning about other cultures. We've had our whole lives regimented, and this is our first chance to break free. All within the bounds of the law though, of course."

Watchara's eyebrows arched halfway up her forehead. "You want tramp transport."

"I do not!" Nicholas continued walking, not bothering to see if Watchara followed. "Those people are filthy, and if there *was* some crime clinging to the Systems, it'd be with them. My sister did six months with one. She came back with botflies. Botflies! Like, the actual Earth bug, but apparently it got off Earth and infested some other world— and found her! And the language the pilots use!"

"You could have mine, if you wanted." A half smile played on Watchara's face.

"Your interview? What'll you do, then? You want to try for the law firm?"

She laughed. "No! But I, uh, was thinking—" She nodded to her left at a wide door marked *EXIT* in Common. She lowered her voice and whispered into his ear. "I was thinking I might run."

The words didn't compute. Run where? Run to what? She had a fine life. They all did. She had good scores, she'd get a good Journey placement, and she was free to spend the next two years doing as much or as little as she wanted. Running didn't make any sense. Nicholas wrinkled his nose and turned to face her. "Run where?"

Watchara opened her arms out and raised them above her head in a clap. "Out there! Anywhere! You don't have to go through the offices, you know." She pointed to the *YOUTH* embroidery. "You got the coveralls, you got the pass."

"Yeah, but you've got to be signed to someone. You can't just be on your own. Right? Youths can't just be unassigned?"

"We get a two-week grace period. We're supposed to be learning ourselves and figuring out adulthood, and what better way than on my own?"

"You could get—"

"Killed? Maimed? Robbed? It's the *Charted Systems*, Nicholas. When was the last time you even yelled at someone?"

"I'm about to."

Watchara smirked. "I'm going. Plenty of offices in this district alone, and I'm sure someone wants cheap labor. Catch you later, trader. Have fun with your books." She sidestepped to the exit door and, with a salute, slipped out into the acidic-smelling air of Corieus's capital.

The door slammed shut behind her. Nicholas let the air curl up into his sinuses as he debated. Part of him wanted to chase after her, but she was right. She wasn't in any danger, and she wasn't really breaking any rules. He could go after her, he supposed, but why? Anything out there wasn't going to be better than anything in here. The internship on Risal was a good opportunity. It would pay well. He'd be happy there, right?

"Right," Nicholas said out loud. He'd walked without thinking farther down the hall and now stood at a T-junction. To his left, the door to room eighteen stood ajar, the backside of a Risalian in a yellow tunic sticking out from the frame. To the right was door seventeen. It was closed, and no light spread from the gap near the floor, but Nicholas could still hear the sounds of arguing.

"Left is security," Nicholas murmured. "Left is security and good wages and probably a good job when I get back to Earth. Right is bugs and hard floors and probably...bars." He bit his lower lip. "Bars and greasy food. Music. Sleeping in till noon and lazy days of reading while you wait to exit a wormhole. Ah, screw it." It was just an interview, right? He could always turn it down.

Nicholas took several short, tentative steps toward the loud voices. The arguing was still going on, but it wasn't angry arguing, like when you accidentally stepped on someone's foot, and they yelled at you for being careless. It was more like when his parents argued about some trivial matter, like his father's inability to see the crumbs he'd left on the countertop. It was mostly indistinct, however, so Nicholas edged to the door and tried to listen in. Best to know what he was walking into before he actually walked into it, surely.

"Well, fuck, Captain. If we can't make the delivery by the ninth, then why take it at all?"

There was a huff and the sound of a chair scooting over a plastic floor. "Because the money is good."

"We won't get paid if we're late!" That voice, the first one, sounded exasperated.

"Maybe we won't be late this time."

Someone sat down heavily on a chair. Nicholas heard the cushion exhale. "When, since I started working for you, have we ever made a delivery on time?"

Well, it certainly sounded like what Nicholas expected. Tramp transport meant hauling jobs for whomever was paying, old, broken-down ships, and crusty space captains. Nicholas wasn't sheltered. He'd watched movies growing up and knew exactly what kind of people, and what kind of smells, in theory, he'd be in for.

"Stupid to be nervous. I need to practice my interview skills anyway," Nicholas murmured before he pushed the door open and stepped in. "I can do this."

"Ah, see? Here is someone now."

Nicholas edged back into the hall as a...well, a biped of some form grabbed his hand with sticky fingers and pulled him to a chair. She was taller than him and had weird little stress lines at the junction where her nose met her forehead. Her hair was strawberry blonde, her skin coppery, and she had way too many fingers. She had to be a Neek, but that didn't make any sense. What was she doing off-world?

"Uhh..." Nicholas began. "Shouldn't you be, I mean, why are you—"

"Sit," the Neek instructed. "I'm asking questions first. How's your sense of time?"

"Uh..." Nicholas looked at the other person in the room. The man was Terran—Nicholas was sure—with a wide, heavyset frame, a little too much paunch than what was considered healthy, and a scruffy, brown beard that was threatening to eat his face and neck. Where it started and where the man's curly, dark-brown hair ended, Nicholas couldn't even begin to discern. He was wearing the same beige flightsuit—wrinkled and stained—as the Neek, and they both smelled exactly as Nicholas had expected. As an added bonus, the Neek's fingers appeared to be dripping some sort of snot. No, wait. Not snot. Mucus. The Neek secreted empathic mucus from their fingers. It was the plot of at least four B movies back on Earth.

"Um. Ah." Nicholas tore his eyes from the Neek's dripping fingers and managed to look at her face. "How might I address you? Captain? Pilot? Madam, sir, or something else?"

The man barked a laugh as the other biped looked startled. Nicholas hunched in his chair. This definitely wasn't the correct way to start an interview. Should he apologize? Laugh along?

"I'm the pilot, and I'm...I'm Neek. A Neek. I don't use modifiers because they're stupid. I'm female, and I... Anyway, my species doesn't do individual names past childhood, so just 'Neek' is fine. This"—she pointed to the Terran—"is Captain Yorden Kuebrich of the tramp transport *Mercy's Pledge*, which is an old-as-dirt space shuttle from your own planet. Captain Kuebrich can tell you about its history better than me."

"You don't use a modifier, so you're just going to use the name of your species and your planet?" Nicholas asked, stupidly, like he was repeating a lesson. "How is that not confusing? You can't just use 'pilot' or something?"

"You don't get an opinion on this," Neek responded acerbically.

"Oh." Nicholas shut his mouth and tried to think before speaking again, but his brain just wasn't connecting with his lips. "You know that 'The Neek Brigade of Jollies' has a worldwide broadcast every Saturday morning around nine AM, right?"

"Jesus," Captain Kuebrich muttered.

Neek's eyebrows rose and remained that way. Earth videos were probably not something she cared about. He needed to get them back on track. "So, what *was* your modifier, then? Before the, well, before?"

Neek's mouth turned down, and she looked away from Nicholas to the wall and stared at it as if she might melt it with her mind.

"Maybe just a little modifier? I could call you, uh, Away Neek, or Ms. Neek, or maybe—"

"Would you shut up?"

Nicholas felt warmth in his cheeks. "I'm sorry!" He stood from his chair. The interview was definitely over.

There was no coming back from whatever he'd just stepped in. Maybe the Risalians were still waiting for him, and he could just slide on over. Hopefully, he didn't already smell like the room he was in.

Captain Kuebrich held out a hand and motioned for him to sit back down. "Call her anything other than 'Neek' and you'll end up with an earful. What do you know about Terran shuttles, kid? Or transport, for that matter?"

Nicholas tried to catch Neek's eyes so he could apologize, but she steadfastly refused to look at him. Frustrated and feeling more than a little guilty, Nicholas sat back in his chair and tried to focus on the captain's questions. "I, um, know a bit about early Earth shuttles, like how some have been modded with cellulose biometals so they can travel outside our solar system. We had a whole unit on it in school. The Earth shuttles have decent cargo space if you didn't mod out the living quarters too much, so I assume you haul small to medium jobs, just..." Nicholas tried to pick his words carefully. "Just, you probably don't haul them very fast."

"Ha. Well, you're not wrong. We need another pair of hands. Neek is my pilot, but the *Pledge* has a combination manual and interface control panel, so Neek's at that ninety percent of the time we're in flight. Thank god for her big hands, because no one else can fly both systems simultaneously. I do most of the repairs—well, the small repairs—but, as you noted, the ship is old, and if something breaks or blows while we're docking or whatever, there's no one to actually make the delivery." Captain Kuebrich shoved his hands into two very large pockets and stood. "You'd be manual labor, mostly. Loading and unloading. We have lots of dead time when we're in wormholes though, so I can walk you through ship maintenance or Neek can teach you some piloting to help meet the mentorship component of Youth Journey."

"I don't have the patience to teach children to fly antiques." Neek still wasn't looking at him, but she was glaring at the captain now. Nicholas had to suppress a laugh because, while Neek's face looked like she meant to physically harm someone, the captain's merely looked amused. Maybe she was just mad a lot. Not having a name might do that to a being.

"We can work out the details later. Do you have any questions for us, Mister St. John?"

The hair rose on Nicholas's arm. Thank heavens his skin was too dark to show a blush. *Mister.* He'd never been called that before, and it seemed really out of place, especially coming from the mouth of a tramp captain. It...it sounded like they were going to offer him this job. Even scarier, Nicholas was almost certain that if they *did* offer, he would accept.

"You—you're aboveboard, right?" Nicholas asked. His voice wavered, so he balled his fists and ground his knuckles into the plastic of his chair. *Professional,* he thought to himself. *Have to be professional, no matter how weird they are, 'cause this is maybe sort of a cool job. It's better than law. Mom'll freak, but that's okay.*

Captain Kuebrich raised an eyebrow, and Neek finally turned to look at him, an unreadable expression on her face.

"I've never been arrested," Yorden said, looking Nicholas right in the eyes.

"That's not really an answer."

"I have," Neek said. "It's not something I wish to repeat."

"Still not answering my question."

"We're not *illegal*," Yorden managed to choke out. Nicholas was certain there was a smile pulling at the captain's mouth. "We, uh, well, we do a lot of jobs for the Markin Council on Risal."

Nicholas blinked. They hauled for the Charted Systems sheriffs? That had to be okay then. The Risalians were the ones who upheld peace across the systems. They ran Cell-Tal, and the ruling council just before the current one had been the ones to mandate Journey in the first place. Thinking about Cell-Tal made Nicholas's heart race. He'd love to get his hands on some of the new biometals being manufactured by the Risalian company. Rumors in the tech sphere said they were maybe a decade away from faster-than-light travel! The cellulose content of metal like that though, or even bioplastic... Nicholas could feel the slight warmth under his fingers. Getting a chance to see Cell-Tal goods before they hit market was definitely worth the time on a tramp transport, even with someone as sticky as a Neek.

"How many hauls do you do for the Markin in a given cycle?" he asked.

Captain Kuebrich blinked rapidly. He turned to Neek, who merely inclined her head toward Nicholas. "Five or six maybe, depending on need," the captain replied. "Rest of the time, we fill in with other, smaller runs. We've got a hold full of andal saplings right now, if you want to see. They're transplants from Neek—that we had to get via courier because someone can't keep her mouth shut— destined for one of Risal's moons. And yeah, I see your face. Andal growth struggles as much as you think it might off Neek, but hey, they keep paying us, so we keep moving them."

"Somewhat slower than the Markin would like," Neek added. "And all I did was send a short, encrypted message. Could have been from anyone. Not my fault the Neek are paranoid." Her posture relaxed. This time, when Nicholas tried to catch her eye, she held his gaze and then flicked a finger toward him. A droplet of her finger-mucus landed on his hand.

"Oh god, *why*?" Nicholas scrubbed the back of his hand on the leg of his coveralls. A funny tickle ran down his spine, and he scrunched up his shoulders.

Neek snorted. She brushed her hands across her pants, and little white flakes fell onto the floor.

Yorden gave Neek a tired look. "After we deliver these, we'll get loaded with a bunch of the new biofilms for Baltec, in the Minoran System. Stuff is so fresh you can still smell the andal sap. What do you say? Want to sign on?"

Did he? Nicholas sat silently for a moment. Two years was a long time on a no-name ship with two no-name people. Still, the thought of the Cell-Tal products pulled at him. He was a tech geek, after all. He had half a dozen pocket communicators in his duffle, and those were just the ones he'd thought might be fun to toy with once he got settled down. Some were old enough to still be called "phones." A few he'd built himself. Getting to look at the brand-new Cell-Tal tech, maybe getting to even meet some of those engineers…it was too good to pass up.

He could take an internship at Cell-Tal and spend two years doing grunt work on the off chance he might be picked to work on one of the new projects, but on a tramp…on a tramp, he'd get to go right to the heart of the manufacturing. They'd be in and out of warehouses all the time. Engineers would have to check the products after they were loaded to make sure no damage had occurred. Nicholas would be alone—well, alone with Captain Kuebrich and Neek—with a cargo hold of Cell-Tal products and a Cell-Tal engineer or two. And if there happened to be a holdup for departure, or some issue with export permits, Nicholas might find the time to wander off the ship and into the labs…

"I'll do it."

Wow, he sounded confident. This was what it was like to be an adult, maybe. Making choices. Turning down one avenue that was definitely what your parents wanted to pursue your dreams. His mother would have a fit. If Hayley had come back from Journey swearing like a sailor from the far reaches of the Systems, then Nicholas couldn't imagine what type of education was in store for him with these two.

"Great." Yorden slapped his thigh as he stood. "I'll go sign the paperwork. Neek will take you to the *Pledge* and get you settled in."

A big grin settled across Neek's face. As Nicholas followed Yorden out the door, Neek slapped Nicholas on the back. She let her hand linger there, and Nicholas felt the wetness from her fingers soak through his coveralls and start to gel on his skin.

"Gaahhh!" He ducked away from her and moved farther down the hall. "Why?"

Neek shrugged and put her hands in her pockets. "Because it's fun—and Terrans seem to uniformly hate *stuk*. Not my problem, but it's definitely going to be yours."

"Do you have to ooze so much?" Nicholas growled as he and Neek took a left while Yorden headed to the main offices.

"Are you really this delicate?" she shot back. They rounded another corner and went out an exit door. There, on a small landing pad, sat a Terran shuttle—a *Soviet* Terran shuttle. It was white, mainly, and most of its external plating had been replaced with basic cellulose weave. There were dents and missing pieces across most of the structure, and near the viewscreen, he saw...a laser turret? Really? Weapons were banned across the Systems. This one looked old enough to have maybe gotten grandfathered in, but still. What kind of Markin haul jobs required *weapons*?

"Jeez," Nicholas muttered as he stared at the shuttle.

"That the best expletive you have?" Neek sighed and slapped at something in her pocket. A boarding ramp extended from the *Pledge*'s side. "We've got a lot of work to do with you. I can see that already. Starting with your vocabulary."

Subversion

2060 CE

Spaceports. They smelled the same no matter what galaxy you were in. This one, at least, had a biometal base, so Corccinth could rip a hole in its side and let herself be sucked into the void if the smell got too bad. The permeating odors of bipedal bodies, Oorin mining fumes, and the red, sticky liquid under her foot was worse than that of burnt andal. Hopefully, she wouldn't be here long, listening to a supposedly pleasant fake water feature as every sort of fur, hair, and scale streaked past.

Corccinth ran bony fingers through her graying hair and then patted her cheeks to check that her thick makeup—the powder that hid her flare markings—was still in place. Most of the beings in the Charted Systems were bipeds, so she was certain she didn't stand out, but that didn't help the restless feeling she had of being a predatory *nhu* in a *titha* breeding ground.

"Advisor Corccinth?"

"You're late. I don't appreciate that." The query had come in Risal's primary language. Corccinth had responded in High Uklam. Not only were all the Risalian languages hard on her throat, but there was no chance that any random passersby would know her native tongue.

A thin Risalian—all elbows, knees, and gill slits, dressed in a light-blue tunic that was far too large for hir frame—sat down tentatively to Corccinth's left on the wobbly wooden bench. It wouldn't have been wobbly if it had been made from andal. Instead, the wood was red with cream-colored streaks and smelled like pesticide. It was another fine example of why Ardulum had never returned to the Charted Systems.

"My apologies," the Risalian responded in near-fluent High Uklam. Impressed, Corccinth straightened. She knew second *dons* on Ardulum that didn't speak High Uklam that well. "My class ran long, and my crèche mates were detained. I'm afraid I'm the only one who can meet with you today. I'm Pihn, a markin trainee. I've been the one corresponding with you via deep-space comm. I know you've come a long way. Might I suggest we go someplace less noisy? I've booked a meeting room on the fortieth floor, and I can have cooked andal brought in for you."

Corccinth's stomach growled, but she frowned. "Tempting, but I have less than two Ardulan hours to return before my next meeting. This isn't an authorized trip, as you might imagine. So, here will do. It gives me a"—she gestured to the three Oori slicks that were sloshing about near her feet—"a feel for the climate, as you might say, of your situation. I don't suppose..."

An unsettling presence flitted across her mind. The hair on Corccinth's arm stood on end as she scanned the area, searching for its owner. The touch hadn't been alien at all, but disjointed. Fragmented. Uncannily familiar.

"Where?" she breathed, but then the presence was back, connecting in a solid lock. Corccinth's eyes followed the invisible mental thread to a shadowed corner. All she could see was a pair of feet streaked with dark veins, but that was more than enough. The presence's voice—a man's—turned sharp. Turned pleading. There were no words, only images of cells and hands and the sounds of harsh voices and screaming.

Corccinth shut down her telepathy, her heart pounding, yelling at herself to just take that poor man and put him on her ship, consequences be damned, and fly them both away from the poison of the Charted Systems.

Fly them away from one death trap—and right back into another.

She stood and took a step forward, pointing to the man. "How many are here, on this station?" she asked when her voice finally returned. Her throat still felt thick, the words burning in her mouth as she spoke them.

Pihn stood as well but looked at the floor, and in hir slumped shoulders and hollow cheeks, she saw hir youth and how little hope they both had for what they were trying to accomplish. "Thirteen, at last count. Callis is our biggest system, and the Callis Spaceport our main hub for the Systems. There are over two million beings in this station at any given moment. It's a terrible strain on the Ardulans, but they...manage."

Corccinth could only cringe. That seemed like a near-impossible amount, even for a flare.

"For comparison, we usually have seventy-five assigned to any given planet, just for general peace purposes. However, there's a lot more that goes on at a spaceport where species routinely interact, so only the most experienced Ardulans are stationed here. Of course, not all the systems need a few Science Talents assigned to them. The Neek, in particular, are so insular that we basically leave them alone. There's only one off-world, and she's kept on a short leash." Pihn snorted. "Earth, though. We've got our hands full with Earth."

Corccinth bit her lower lip. "How long, in your estimation, has the Risalian government used them as pacifiers? What kind of chaos will it cause if they were to disappear en masse instead of slowly?"

Pihn looked up at her and rubbed at hir neck slits. "The last component of the Ardulan project was installed in 2040. They'd been tinkering around with it since 1880."

She looked at hir with exasperation. A light-blue tunic xe might have had, but Pihn was one hundred percent Risalian egocentrism. "I have no idea what those numbers mean."

Pihn's neck tinged purple. "Of course. Sorry. I don't know how to convert it to your calendar. The Charted Systems adopted the Terran calendar when they joined. It was part of the negotiation process, and none of the other systems really cared about such a trivial thing as date keeping. But to answer your question, the Systems weren't ready for this level of peace. It's so artificial, you can practically smell it. If you were to take the Ardulans back now, all of them, the Systems would fall apart. And I don't think it would be long before it spilled over into the

Alliance—especially given the perpetual border skirmishes the Risalians have with the Mmnnuggls."

Mmnnuggls. Bah. Corccinth sniffed and waved a dismissive hand. "The Mmnnuggls can be dealt with easily enough, or used where appropriate. What I'm hearing from you, Pihn, is that it will take years to recover my people. I don't *have* years. Ardulum has been rumbling of a move for months now. We have maybe two years at most before it gets up enough energy—or whatever it is the planet needs—to move to a new system." She narrowed her eyes and pointed again at the dark corner containing the man she refused to mentally touch again. If she did, it would split her apart.

"You're in a bad place to make demands," Pihn said defensively. "It was your people that sold the defective Ardulans to us in the first place."

She really wanted to smack hir across those silly gill slits. "They are *not* defective!" Three Minorans stopped their chatting on the other end of the circular plaza to stare. Corccinth hissed at them, and their ears twitched as they turned back to their own conversation. "They are not defective unless you made them that way."

"*I'm* not part of the genetics operations, nor do I work for Cell-Tal. I'm here to help you, so I don't appreciate your anger. I agree that your people, unwilling or not, should not be here. I dislike how much the Markin Council relies on their abilities, especially noting their declining birth rates and general poor health. If I could gather them all and put them on a transport home, I would. But that just isn't possible."

"Well, what *is* possible? Why did you invite me here if only to tell me that man in the corner is lost?"

Pihn took a deep breath, reached into hir pocket, and pulled out a thin, rolled tablet. Xe handed it to Corccinth. "Because of this. One of my crèche mates is interning at Cell-Tal. They've made a new variant. The genetics of the girl are on the tablet."

Corccinth unrolled the film with jittery hands. She and Pihn had been in contact for months, and the data xe had sent on the Risalian genetic tinkering of the Ardulan flares was so disturbing that Corccinth had not been able to read the files on a full stomach. With the flare in the corner, his mental pleading batting at her mind, she wasn't certain she could focus at all on the biofilm.

Because really, this was all Ardulum's fault. They could play the blame game, but in the end, it was the Ardulans who had stranded their kin here in the first place. The previous Eld had needed to decrease the mental load on the planet when they left Neek's orbit, well over one hundred years ago. Traditional protocol was to cull the flares—the Ardulans who manifested more than two Talents and were generally deemed unstable—but the Risalians had offered a better option. Mentally gelding them, the Eld had stripped them of their Talents, every last one, and sold them to the Risalians, presenting them as mute beasts of burden with limited intellect.

It was appalling. It was nauseating. It was planned. It was methodical.

It was *wrong*.

And the Risalians had only made it worse. Corccinth unrolled the film and grimaced. This...the genetic code she was looking at right now shouldn't have even been *possible*. She could only begin to imagine how the Talent structure of this child would manifest, and every imagining she had ended in mass destruction. And the girl's *mind*...andal help her.

"She cannot be brought up by Risalians." Corccinth spat the words, flecks of spittle landing on the film and absorbing into the cellulose.

"I know." Pihn took the tablet back, rolled it, and placed it back into hir pocket. "Cell-Tal keeps her in containment with her progenitor on a ship in constant movement. They don't want her anywhere near the Risalian homeworld until she's manifested, and they can do testing. She's still a few months out from second *don*. Thus far, developing normally."

"She won't, with those changes. You've stripped off all of our protections, as well as all the naturally occurring genetic checks, like limited telepathy after first *don*. None of the Talent genes are silenced."

Pihn suddenly looked like a *titha* that had been kicked one too many times. "And I think Cell-Tal may have found a few new ones, too. My people have gotten too used to controlling populations, and the Mmnnuggl pestering bothers them more than it should. She will be a weapon— more so than any of the others."

Corccinth cursed and balled her fists into the fabric of her long skirt. Andal *damn* the Risalians! "How hard would it be to get her off that ship?"

Pihn shook hir head. "Violence would likely be necessary. Likely the ship would have to be destroyed. You're forgetting, too, her age. If the ship goes under attack and something happens to the mother..."

Corccinth didn't bother filling in the rest. It was touching, in a way, that Pihn was so concerned for the girl's survival, but the problem could resolve itself, it seemed, should an attempt to capture the girl fail. She found that comforting, if not morbid, but there were hundreds of flare lives at stake, as well as billions of beings in the Charted Systems. Corccinth trained flares—the ones that had been born since the move—back on Ardulum. While she didn't like their containment, she did understand its purpose. Until they learned how to deal with all that raw power, they were a danger to themselves and everyone around them. And this girl, *this girl*, was a nuclear reactor with a gelded mind. She was a *titha* with an intergalactic laser. Death would be a mercy.

Corccinth unfurled her fingers and smoothed the wrinkles on her skirt. "I have some people that work for me who could disintegrate that ship. I can have them here in three days. We can deal with this issue now and then, after the fallout, return to our original goal."

"I would prefer a different course." Pihn's neck was now bright purple. Corccinth couldn't ascertain why. Xe had shown her the tablet, after all. Pihn understood the ramifications of such a child. She wasn't a pet. She was barely Ardulan, at this point, with all the Risalian tinkering. They were in this to save lives, weren't they?

Pihn pulled a laser gun from hir satchel. It was an oddly shaped thing, with a barrel that seemed too long for regular use. "Do you know much about tramp transport, Advisor?"

"No." Corccinth wrinkled her nose and tapped two fingers on the black biometal exterior of the gun. "Trade comes to us. We don't generally go to it."

Pihn nodded and placed the gun back in its satchel. "The Markin have allowed a small number of vessels to remain outside our Ardulan influence—and marginally outside our laws. The reasoning is somewhat complex, but generally, it revolves around our negotiations with the Neek and their distrust of technology. These beings serve, too, as a sort of touchstone for where the Systems are without Risalian influence. They're a way to check in, I think. See if we can ease up on the influence. The Risalian endgame is *true* peace, not a manufactured one, but that takes time. A lot of beings have to forget a lot of old grudges." Xe pointed. "Walk with me?"

Corccinth nodded, and Pihn led her around several Oori puddles, toward the sound of the fake waterfall. "I don't follow," Corccinth called up to hir. "Are you concerned about an early removal of the flares unraveling the 'good' your people have done for the Charted Systems?"

Pihn shook hir head but, after a moment, turned back around and frowned. "Yes, to a degree. But also, I want to suggest an alternative. We have beings, Advisor, who could help integrate this girl. They would care for her and her mother—of that, I am sure. There is one ship in particular that has the cultural background necessary—and the contact network—to hide the child until she is old enough to make her own choices."

Corccinth frowned as they went around a bend to a central plaza with not one but *three* artificial water features. Of course. "According to your reports, your Ardulans don't *make* choices. They don't have free will. Did Cell-Tal change that, too?"

Pihn guided her to the left. "No, but I'm not convinced that narrative is entirely true. They're still sentient, just resigned. One cannot make choices when there are no choices to make. If the girl grows up in a moral void, what choices will she make when she breaks free of containment? We both agree that the Risalians are not capable of holding someone of her potential. When they try to keep her contained, or when they separate her from her mother, there will be violence. She will *learn* violence."

They approached a small alcove surrounded by holographic andal trees, the sound of falling water clearly echoing from a speaker in the wall. Pihn inclined hir head. In the alcove sat a large, bushy Terran and a smaller, better-groomed one. They were huddled over a tablet, occasionally making emphatic gestures. Both wore stained and torn beige flightsuits, and the woman, in particular, wore thick-soled boots, which was rare to see in the Systems. Especially on Terrans. They did love their fashion.

Corccinth sent a questioning look to Pihn. Xe motioned to keep walking and waited until they were a good distance away before responding.

"They haul for Cell-Tal," xe responded. "Primarily to Neck."

Corccinth's eyes opened wide in understanding. "Not a Terran. She's *the* Neek, then? The only one off-world?"

"Yes. Kicked off her planet because she thinks Ardulum is a fairy tale meant to keep her people from the stars."

A bubble of laughter burst from Corccinth's mouth. This was, well, this was *delicious*. "This is why we've stopped seeding in primitive cultures. Gives the Eld big heads." She paused then, considering. As amusing as it would be to drop a child god on a Neek, the situation did require some delicacy. Corccinth carefully formed her next question. "You want to drop a genetically modified Ardulan on a heretic Neek and a Terran tramp captain? These are the morals you want that girl to have?"

"Yes." Pihn toyed with hir satchel. Xe took a deep breath and exhaled through hir slits, which eased their coloring into a shade closer to gray. "Anyone else would figure out what that girl can do and turn her over to us. Law-abiding citizens, remember? Ardulans tinkering with their minds. But give her to a Neek with enough entrenched dogma to continuously deny what the girl is and a Terran who cares about galactic politics about as much as he cares about combing his hair?" Xe looked up. "They're perfect."

Corccinth chewed the inside of her lip, considering, as they walked past yet another holographic waterfall. Having the girl and her mother loose in the Systems for a good number of years...there were a lot of things that could go wrong in that scenario. "You're not concerned at all about the effect of having two free Ardulans in the Systems when you have your hidden ones everywhere? If they're making mental connections with me, surely they will with her as well."

Pihn's gaze remained steadily on Corccinth. Xe didn't look away, but hir neck had completely reverted to blue. Xe stopped in the middle of the walkway, forcing dozens of beings to weave around them. Hir shoulders were squared, hir breath calm.

"That's the plan then, is it?" Corccinth asked, coming up next to hir. "Instead of the Systems' destruction, you want to engineer the salvation of the Risalian Ardulans?"

For a moment, it looked like Pihn might deflate, but the moment passed and hir confidence returned. "If we do nothing, we are guaranteed destruction. If we do this, then there is a small chance for stability. For your people to go home, to let the Charted Systems find their own peace, and for that girl to have a real life."

Corccinth's stomach rumbled again. She had a piece of cooked andal in the pocket of her skirt, but she refrained from reaching for it. The hunger kept her sharp when everything in this conversation was pushing her toward foolish hope. It was impossible, this chain of events that Pihn proposed, but then, she lived on a traveling, sentient planet. She could do things most beings would consider magic. Who was she to say there was no hope? It wasn't her planet that was being gambled with, nor any of the Alliance.

"How do we start this into motion?"

Pihn took the gun from the satchel and held it out to Corccinth. "It's a stun gun, mostly. Works across species, but it blocks Ardulan Talents, too. Here. Take it."

She took it, and Pihn led them, wordlessly, through another hall to a small storefront. Above the wide door, in neon letters, the sign read, *SPACE STUFF!!*

"Charming," she muttered. Louder, she said, "Contraband, I take it?"

Pihn reached into hir satchel and removed a gray tunic. Xe pulled Corccinth to the side into a small alcove where xe removed hir light-blue tunic, folded it neatly into a triangle, and placed it into the satchel. The gray tunic that went onto Pihn's bony frame was much better fitting, although it was stained around the collar and had a frayed hem. Pihn unclasped hir black hair from the bun on hir head and raked fingers through the strands, mussing them into knots. Xe gestured to Corccinth to return the gun, opened hir eyes wide enough that xe looked like a comically frightened child, and then turned back toward the shop's entrance.

"They shop here, I take it?"

Pihn nodded. "Not frequently, and maybe not this trip. Maybe not the next. But eventually, they're going to come in here and see this gun. They'll buy it because Neek—that Neek anyway—loves weapons, and Captain Kuebrich has a thing for history. It'll come with information about a desperate Risalian, which will be something that will stew in Captain Kuebrich's mind. They'll get the gun analyzed. No one will have seen anything like it. They'll follow the breadcrumbs."

"You think they have the capacity to attack a Risalian frigate and rescue the mother and child?"

Pihn straightened hir tunic—even though there was no amount of straightening that would remove the wrinkles—and started into the shop. Over hir shoulder, xe called, "No, not them. That's the part where I need your help. How well do you know the Mmnnuggls?"

The Gift of Friendship

First Month of Squinth, 1_16

"Corccinth said this shop would be fine. Would you just come on?" Nicholas gestured impatiently as he held open a thin, wooden door for Emn. Just beyond were tables heaped with clothes—because shelving in a storefront was a Terran thing, apparently. Knives, on the other hand, were universal, since on the wall behind the bored-looking proprietor hung three or four dozen of the things, many of which had a curve to the blade that made Nicholas's hair stand on end. Maybe Emn wouldn't notice?

"I think we should just keep walking. It's hot, anyway. Maybe we should go back and get some water." Emn tugged up the collar of her shirt and then pulled down the cuffs of the sleeves. Unnecessary, Nicholas thought, because she was wearing gloves, too. Only her face was uncovered by the thick, black cotton she wore, and so the two upside-down triangles under her eyes—thick, dark veins showing through her skin—were hard to miss. It was hotter than Minnesota in July, with just as many irritating insects, so while Nicholas didn't envy the neck-to-ankle flightsuit, he did covet the coverage. Someone needed to make a galactic law against bugs.

"It'll be fine, Emn. Come *on*."

He grabbed her hand, and she finally acquiesced. For someone who had begged for help in picking out a gift for Atalant, Emn was certainly hesitant to actually go into a shop. Nicholas understood, of course—native Ardulans were pretty much galactic jerks—but if Emn wanted to shop within a day of traveling by ground transport, they didn't have many options. Most of the commerce on the small northwestern continent of Ardulum had been at the capital and, well, that was just construction now that Nicholas had somehow been put in charge of. Thannon, where they were currently residing, had a decent number of shops, but they were pretty touristy. Emn had walked right past the last six, but Corccinth had suggested this one by name. Besides, Nicholas was hot. They needed a chance to cool down.

Emn pulled the door firmly shut behind them, keeping out a hot breeze. The proprietor didn't bother to greet them, nor did he look up from his biofilm, which was just par for the course.

Nicholas cleared his throat. The proprietor pushed his biofilm aside in exaggerated agitation and glared at Nicholas.

"What?"

"Guns?" Nicholas asked in halting High Uklam.

The proprietor continued to glare.

He was pretty certain he'd said the word right, but just in case, Nicholas tried Common. "Can you tell us about your, uh, guns? You know, *pew pew*?" He made an L shape with his thumb and forefinger and pointed to a cluster of small handguns tacked to the south wall. Emn groaned.

The proprietor's eyes snapped to Emn. Her stance went rigid. Then, in another heartbeat, a smile broke across his face. The edge of the counter, which Nicholas suspected had started turning to cellulose dust, stabilized.

"Ah! Apologies! It's been, well, weird, lately. As you know, I'm sure. But a flare is always welcome in my shop. What can I get you?"

"Thank god for Common," Nicholas murmured before turning to Emn. Louder, he said, "So, uh, what *were* you thinking of, specifically?"

Emn studied the gun above Nicholas's head, which looked a lot like a Risalian stun gun. Nicholas smiled at the memory of Atalant shooting him with one back at Chen's shop in the Charted Systems. He remembered how angry he'd been, and how she always seemed so mad at him, and how he never seemed to know the right things to say. But, thinking about it now...it *was* pretty funny. He hadn't known anything about anything, and now he was on a sentient planet, helping a god pick out a gift for another god—not that either would appreciate being called that.

"I was thinking something unique," Emn drawled as she worked her way around the shop. She poked at small pistols, riot rifles, knives of every variety, and a surprising collection of handcuffs that didn't look like they were for criminal restraint. "Maybe something that isn't actually lethal."

"From any system in particular? I have stock from fourteen systems, as well as historic pieces from Ardulum's past." The proprietor wove between two tables to stand in front of them. He smelled like spring andal sap, and Nicholas could see traces of his breakfast still dotting the corners of his mouth. Or, wait, no. Not sap, but something sticky and clumpy all the same. Makeup?

Nicholas tugged on Emn's sleeve and pointed before he had the chance to consider whether he was being rude. "Hey, Emn?"

Emn turned, blinked, and then her mouth dropped open in understanding. "Oh. Corccinth—"

The proprietor snorted. "Recommended my shop? Not surprised. Still, makeup would be a lot more cooling than the getup you have, Emn. But I guess everyone knows you. There doesn't seem to be much point in hiding."

"You're still hiding," Nicholas countered.

The proprietor snorted. "Old habits are hard to break. I'm working on it."

"Yeah," Emn said with a sigh. "Me too." She leaned heavily against the wall, the side of her head just brushing the handle of what was almost certainly a Dulan knife.

"Here, then. In the spirit of kinship." The proprietor used his long sleeves to wipe off most of the makeup from his face. His skin was a tawny copper underneath, and the triangular markings on his face were impossible to ignore. "I'm Mithal." He stuck his hand out, sideways. Emn raised her eyebrows.

"It's how Terrans greet each other. I don't know what Risalian Ardulans do. I didn't want to offend."

Mithal was definitely one of the friendliest Ardulans Nicholas had met—or else the quickest to warm up to them—but he hadn't had a chance to hang out with many of Corccinth's flares, either. In the spirit of not being mean to someone who'd been given the short end of the stick his whole life, Nicholas shook Mithal's hand. "Pleasure. I'm Nicholas St. John. I'm from a part of Earth that only uses one last name, although I have two middle names. Well, I guess my last name is also two words. Uh. It's a little superfluous."

Emn let out a long breath and then shook Mithal's hand as well. "And I'm Emn, as you no doubt know."

"Yes, the only one of us with any clue of how to actually use all these Talents we've got." Mithal let go of her hand and leaned back against the counter. "What a life you must have."

"I guess. I haven't had much time to really think about it." Emn peeled the gloves from her hands and unzipped the front of her flightsuit to her collarbones.

"Nice," Nicholas said, tapping her bare hand. "This is good progress."

Emn shrugged.

"So, is the gift for anyone in particular?" Mithal looked pointedly at Emn. "Perhaps an eld?"

Nicholas grinned at her.

Emn blushed. "Um. Yes."

"Eld Atalant is it, then?"

Emn nodded, but still didn't speak, so Nicholas chimed in. "Yes, Eld Atalant. We were thinking a belated birthday gift, especially with the whole ascending business." He leaned toward the proprietor. "What *is* an appropriate gift for that? What do you even call it? Not a birthday, I bet. *Don*-day?   Happy-new-phase-of-life-and-oh-look-at-that-you're-an-eld day?"

Mithal laughed. "So, we don't celebrate birthdays, clearly, since we have *dons*. But I know the Neek do, so might I suggest two presents?"

Nicholas saw Emn cringe. She'd had a *lot* of concerns about finding just one gift, so Nicholas imagined that trying to pick out two gifts that were somehow better than having a whole planet thrust at your feet was pretty overwhelming.

Nicholas put his hand on her upper arm. "You okay?"

Emn nodded. "Just don't want to screw this up," she murmured back. "Can you help?"

"Of course. That's what I'm here for." Turning back to Mithal, Nicholas asked, "Are we supposed to buy gifts related to the Talent, or is that, like, in bad taste?"

"Well now, that depends on if you want to follow older traditions or modern ones. We're a few millennia past literal sacrifices, but on one of the southern continents— one of the little ones—they still prepare a smoked *illa,* which is a genetic cousin of a *titha,* to present to the new eld. Each region has its own marinade, and the eld has to try each one and pronounce a 'winner.' In contrast, the capital city..."

Nicholas tried really hard to pay attention, but he was still exhausted. Ardulum had moved, what, four days ago? Atalant was an eld, she and Emn had almost figured themselves out, but no one had had a moment of peace because there were angry, sentient fungi dangling from every surface and a million demands on their time. Heck, Atalant had put *him* in charge of palace reconstruction because she didn't have time. Nicholas didn't know how to build a palace! The closest he'd ever gotten was a sandcastle when he was ten for which he'd managed to build an underground moat.

"...regardless of region. On a personal level, a freshly minted second *don* would get gifts from their family that align with their Talent. We don't normally gift anything for third *don,* but that isn't to say it doesn't happen. It's just not as big a deal since there's no big transformation." He scratched his chin. "Most Ardulans just wake up feeling...different. Something resets or changes in our body. And for Eld..." He barked a laugh. "You got me there! There are usually ceremonies for an ascension, but they're private, and common people would never just be invited."

He met Emn's eyes. "Corccinth would have gone to plenty. She didn't have any ideas?"

"She sent us here! So, I guess, here is where we shop." Nicholas put his hands on his hips and nodded at Emn. "Pick something." If he'd had telepathy, he'd have considered adding, *Probably not a Dulan knife. That seems in bad taste.*

"You've known her longer than I have, Nick," Emn tried to argue. "I don't know what kind of gun she likes."

"Heeeeey." Nicholas took a step back. "Don't pin this on me. We're here because you wanted to get her a gift. A gun seems like a good idea. That's all I ever saw her shop for. She used to have quite a collection on the *Pledge,* and I'm sure she wouldn't mind restarting the hobby, even if she doesn't have much free time."

Emn hunched her shoulders. "I'd prefer we at least didn't get her a weapon historically used to kill my side of the gene pool."

Nicholas nodded. "Fair, fair." He turned to Mithal. "What about, like, a really *big* gun?" He held his hands about a meter apart. "*Substantial.* But also, something historic because I really don't see her needing to shoot the thing what with the controlling the andal and all. Or with the andal controlling you all—however it works."

"You don't sell alcohol by any chance, do you?" Emn asked abruptly. "Whiskey, right, Nicholas? Isn't that what she and Yorden drink? It smells like window cleaner."

Nicholas nodded. "Yes, but I don't think 'single malt Scotch whiskey' is going to translate well. High Uklam is okay, but it's not so...specific."

"Liquor?" Mithal perked up. "I've got plenty of that. Come on back."

Emn looked questioningly at Nicholas, but he just shrugged and followed the man back behind the counter and into a dimly lit room beyond. Liquor was a galactic currency, Yorden had always told him. Always good in a pinch when your rounds were low. He'd claimed that he'd never been to a spaceport or planet where some couldn't be found within an hour, even if most of it was pretty low quality. Yorden had been big on training Nicholas's palate before, well, everything.

Nicholas heard a snap before the small room flooded with light. Reality seemed to slip into the shadows. Covering the floor and dangling from the ceiling on twine were more bottles of alcohol than Nicholas had ever seen.

"You...collect a lot," Nicholas said, drawing out each word as he stared, gaping, at the room. "Is that...is that from *Earth*?"

Nicholas pointed to an empty bottle the length of Emn's arm. Squinting, he read, "Glenfiddich 21."

"What does it mean?" Emn asked.

"It's from *Earth*," Nicholas said. "Scotland!"

"We travel," Mithal said smugly. "I trade."

"Jesus," Nicholas muttered.

"Would she like it?" Emn asked. "Is it strong? The few times we've had alcohol, it's always dulled her telepathy enough that she couldn't hear as many andal trees. This might work well."

Nicholas could almost taste the highland whiskey, could almost hear Captain Kuebrich pouring the amber liquid into a thick glass and demanding Nicholas tell him what he could smell. Nicholas hadn't even been on the *Pledge* for a year when it was destroyed. What memories would Atalant have from one of Captain Kuebrich's signature drinks? Forget drowning out the andal. Toasting to Yorden's memory was an amazing idea.

"Atalant'll drink basically anything, but Yorden loved that brand. I think it's a really good choice."

Emn straightened, but her face seemed to relax. "I like the idea of a Yorden tribute. We'll take it."

Mithal grunted good-naturedly and twisted his way back through shaking stacks. "Head back up front. Going to take me a minute. That's just an empty show bottle. If you're looking for a second gift, there's plenty to dig through while I get the real one."

Nicholas followed Emn to the door, scanning the rows and rows of bottles as they went. "They have at least four Mars whiskies here, too," he whispered. "I think I saw something from Neek as well. Can you imagine? Once everything settles down, we could have, like, actual parties!"

"That sounds great, Nicholas."

Nicholas pointed at a blue bottle on a shelf above the door as they exited. "I think that one is Oorin! Hey, Emn..."

Emn had gone ahead, back to the main room, and was now wedged between two tall stacks of clothing, sitting cross-legged on the floor. Melancholy seemed to have dropped over her like a wet blanket.

Nicholas slumped beside her. They were back here again, and Nicholas was never sure what to say. Ardulan racism he could give Emn pointers on all day—Earth had never managed to outgrow its biases, either—but the whole Atalant and Emn thing...that was outside his sphere.

"Emn, what's wrong?"

Emn visibly swallowed and put her head on her knees.

Nicholas wrapped an arm around her shoulders and rested his head against hers. She smelled like cinnamon and faintly of sweat, and it reminded him of the Mmnnuggl pod and how much they had talked right after her metamorphosis. They'd both grown a lot since then, but they were still far more alike than different.

"Sometimes, there are things we can't talk about with the people we care the most about. That's why friends exist." Nicholas tangled his fingers into Emn's and squeezed.

"She doesn't need any of this stuff, Nick."

Nicholas nodded. "Birthdays aren't really about what you need."

Emn sat up and turned so she could look directly at Nicholas. "But she has an *entire planet*. If she wanted a"—Emn pointed to the wall with the guns—"knife or an old-period rifle, she could ask one of her thousand attendants who will not leave her alone, and they'd get it to her within the hour." Nicholas started to argue, but Emn cut him off. "I understand that us getting her a present has sentiment behind it, but how do you...how do you commemorate becoming an eld when you weren't even Ardulan to start with? What says, 'we were meant for each other, and fate has a weird sense of humor'?" Emn inclined her head toward the back room, where Nicholas could still hear Mithal moving bottles. "Whiskey? Does whiskey say all that? Or is it just a transparent attempt by me to get her drunk so I can kiss my girlfriend without andal chittering in the background?"

Kissing? That's what this was about? For some reason, Nicholas had assumed they were still in the "I don't know how to talk to you because you're practically my god" phase. Kissing was much more basic. Kissing he could help with.

Nicholas smiled, and he must have looked particularly mischievous because Emn burst into laughter. "What?" she asked.

Nicholas started to point at Emn, but then dropped his hand back and bit his lower lip. He'd have to approach this delicately since Emn had even less experience than he did. "Have you two, uh—" He coughed. "You know. Sex?"

A blush spread from Emn's face to her fingertips. "N-no. Some...lead-up, I guess, but..."

Nicholas swallowed loudly and sat back against a pile of clothes. "So, like, I don't—I mean, you know I'm asexual, and I'm not the hands down galaxy expert on this, but... Have you thought of, you know, maybe?" He balled his hands into fists and knocked them together a few times. "Nothing says 'happy birthday' like, er, nudity. For most people, anyway."

Emn swallowed a laugh. "Nicholas, there hasn't been a moment since Atalant kissed me at the inn in which I *haven't* thought of sex. I haven't stopped thinking about it since I emerged as a second *don*, and now I'm sharing not only a room but also a bed with the woman I love, but I don't know how to, you know. Ask." She paused for a moment before continuing. "I want to. She wants to. We sort of swap emotions on it from time to time, but...I don't know. I guess she's just too busy."

An idea popped into his head. It was half-baked and maybe kind of silly, but there was a big difference between romance and sex, and maybe, just maybe, it was actually brilliant. "There isn't time, or you both feel too awkward about it?" Nicholas asked.

Emn considered. "Maybe both? It seems callous to say, 'Hey so, Atalant, we have ten minutes. Can I rip your robe off and...'" Emn's ears turned red. "I can't even *talk* about sex."

"Ahh." Nicholas pursed his lips together and tried not to smile. The more he thought about his plan, the more he liked it. "What's on her calendar for tonight?"

"Huh? Oh." Emn reached into her back pocket and pulled out a folded biofilm tablet. She tapped it on and scrolled until Atalant's calendar came up. "She's in a meeting with the Eiean Council for the next two hours. Then, she has a dinner here in Thannon as part of the Eld ascension ceremony tour, a fitting for a new robe near the inn, another meeting that's listed as 'just make it stop,' and then some sort of social event she labeled 'Arik meetings and booze pls kill me.'"

"Perfect!" Nicholas shot up, pulling Emn with him. Mithal came out at the same time with the whiskey. Nicholas grabbed the bottle, and Emn was barely able to say a thank you before Nicholas had her out of the store and halfway down the block.

"Nicholas!" Emn said, breathless, as they ran. "You'll break the bottle! Also, we didn't pay!"

"Corccinth said she'd take care of it. Anyway, I have a *brilliant* idea." They rounded a sharp corner, and Nicholas stopped them in front of a small cottage that Emn had already passed over. The bay window in the front had so many books stacked against it that Nicholas couldn't see inside at all, but that didn't matter. If it had paper books, then it had a cellulose printer, and Nicholas had plenty of ready files on his portable comm. The data storage capacity of cellulose was so much higher than anything in Earth's history that Nicholas could, and did, store every piece of media his family owned on his personal device.

"Books?" Emn asked hesitantly as Nicholas pushed the door in and dragged her inside. The smell of dry rot hit them both at the same time, but while Nicholas grimaced, Emn cracked a smile. "Something is using cellulose in here, Nicholas, and it's not me."

"Just hear me out, okay?" He didn't let her go until they were halfway through the shop, in an aisle filled with green paper—paper!—books with little, yellow andal flowers embossed on the spines. "Robe fittings can wait, and clearly, Atalant doesn't want to go to whatever Arik thing she has. I have the perfect idea. We just have to print the right one. Here." He handed Emn the whiskey bottle and flagged down the far-too-cheerful Ardulan smiling at them from the corner of the shop.

"Do you speak Common?" Nicholas asked loudly. No sense bothering with High Uklam. There was no way he could properly translate what he wanted the printer for.

"And seven other languages besides." The tall, thin gatoi approached, zir pale-orange hair braided neatly down zir back, zir skin the same tint as Atalant's. Zie spoke with a slight, smooth accent that seemed to settle Emn's nerves until she looked down at her hands and the collar of her unzipped flightsuit.

"My gloves," Emn squeaked. She immediately turned back to the door. "I left them at the last place. I'll just be a minute."

"Emn, wait." Nicholas grabbed her hand. Emn pulled against him, embarrassment flushing her face. Nicholas scowled. If she left, she'd never come back, and he had no idea where they'd find a book printer—especially one set up specifically for paper—in the capital proper.

"Nicholas, please. I have to go."

"Emn, Corccinth recommended this place too. It should be fine."

Emn stopped pulling and hesitantly looked back at the bookshop assistant. Nicholas looked, too. Zie wore the same smile as before, and it didn't look forced. Still, there was clearly no makeup on zir, either.

"You're welcome here, Emn," zie said, zir voice like syrup. "I've worked with Corccinth for a long time, especially on her flare 'project.' You are safe. You'd be surprised, I think, at how many of us non-flares she's touched."

"See?" Nicholas released her hand. "Okay? And if it isn't, you could destroy zir livelihood in like, one second."

"Comforting," the shopkeeper said. "I appreciate the subtlety."

"Emn, please," Nicholas whispered. "Trust me."

"Okay," Emn relented, keeping her eyes on the assistant. "What are we looking for?"

Nicholas's eyes turned bright. He grinned lopsidedly as he turned back to the assistant. "Is your book printer available for use?"

"Yes," the assistant said, drawing out the syllable, "but we have a wide selection. Did you want to see if what you're after is already printed, first?"

Nicholas waved his hand. "We're after something *old*. Also, something Terran. I've got the file. It'll just take a minute to print."

"You might be surprised." The gatoi pointed to the bottom row of books behind Nicholas. "Take a look."

Nicholas squatted down, Emn behind him, and started thumbing through the titles listed in Common. "Okay, but do Ardulans write books about romance?" He pulled one out, considered the "tentaclawed" quadruped in lingerie on the cover, and hastily shoved it back in. "Biped romance, that is. You know, person meets another person, or two, I guess, since you all do threesomes regularly. But circumstances keep them apart, but then, in the end, there's kissing and maybe some nudity?"

"Nicholas!" Emn hissed.

"It's a thing!"

The assistant chortled. "Of course! You're in our 'Recreation' section right now, and the items on the far right are imported from the Charted Systems, some from Earth, even. We have everything you see in paper also available on bark, biofilm, and numerous metals. Paper is just easier to display."

"Huh. I'm betting you don't have—" But there it was. Sandwiched between a cover with a three-breasted alien biped and a cover with a seething robot horde was his sister's favorite book. The book she'd forced him to read his sophomore year of high school. The book she'd stolen from their dead grandmother's nightstand before their mother could keep it from their delicate little minds. *Passion of the Pitcher Plants: An Old Bog Novel.*

"Nicholas, I do not need a sex book!" Emn hissed at him. "I know *how* to do it, just not how to bring it up."

"Okay, but wait." Nicholas looked up at her, triumphant, and held out the ratty paperback. It was a first printing, the edges of the cover curled. He flipped to the interior pages to check the publishing date: 2030. Solid vintage and solid camp, with the cover showcasing two light-skinned Terran women. One was up to her waist in sand while the other looked to be trying to pull her out. They were dressed completely inappropriately for the forest, wearing strapped dresses. Their hair was long, loose, and flowing, and the one not in the sand was wearing shoes with some sort of spike on the heel. Their breasts were, of course, falling out of their dresses, something that had bothered Nicholas to no end in high school but that would work just perfectly for Emn.

"Just take a look at it, okay?"

Emn took the book with her thumb and forefinger and flipped it. "Nicholas, it looks ridiculous."

"Okay, but just *read* a little bit of it. Imagine reading it to Atalant. Think how much easier it would be to talk to her about...stuff, if you've read about it first."

Emn raised an eyebrow.

"*Try* it. And don't think for a minute that I don't understand romance just because I don't want to stick my penis in another being. Open the whiskey. Have a glass each. Read the chapters aloud."

Emn huffed. "Fine. Where should I start?"

Nicholas flipped through the book until he found the part just before the first sex scene. "Here. The scientist's instruments aren't working in the bog because of...plot convenience, and the hiker has stopped to see if she can help repair them. But the bog mat is fragile, and they could fall in and soak their clothes at any time. And the only backup clothes they have are the evening wear the scientist packed for her formal dinner that night."

Emn squinted at the book, took it between her thumb and forefinger again, and read the passage Nicholas pointed to. "'But just as Emily reached for the spectrophotometer, Mary's foot broke through the bog mat. Mary screamed, tossed the brand-new GPS onto higher ground, and grabbed Emily's arms. "It's *so cold*," she wailed. "Quick, pull me out, and then I've got to get out of these clothes immediately. My jeans are really hard to take off when they're wet, and I don't know how I'll ever get out of them!"'"

"Jeans are pants," Nicholas explained when he caught Emn's confused look. "If you move ahead a page, you'll see that they are, in fact, difficult to remove and—"

"And Emily falls into the bog and has to change her clothes as well," Emn finished for him. She looked up at Nicholas. "Right?"

"Ah, yeah. The plot's kind of obvious. That's the point of a lot of these. You don't really read them for the plot." When Emn continued to look perplexed, Nicholas took the book and set it on the floor. Were there some Ardulan or Risalian mores he was stepping on that Emn somehow knew about but he didn't? He and Emn had had plenty of conversations about body parts and sex stuff during their time on the stolen pod. Why was a conversation with Atalant so different?

"Emn?" He prodded. "It was just an idea. We can try something else."

"No!" Emn grabbed the book, stood, and then crushed it to her chest. "It's, ah— We should definitely get it."

Nicholas rubbed at his forehead. "Now I'm confused. You looked terrified a minute ago."

Emn looked everywhere, ignoring his eyes. "This book is fine, Nicholas. It was a good idea. We can go. We only have a few hours before Atalant is done with her meetings, and the book could use a cleaning before then. Galactic used books are probably pretty gross. The book itself isn't, I'm sure, and using pitcher plants as allegory for...stuff is pretty clever since neither one of them ever tries to do anything sexual with one."

Nicholas's mouth fell open. He snapped it shut and narrowed his eyes. "But there is a gross part when Mary kicks what she thinks is a bog body and then they both fall into quicksand, right?"

Emn laughed nervously and tugged on Nicholas's shirt until he stood. "Definitely not as gross as that scene. Can we go?"

"You've read this before!" Nicholas crowed triumphantly.

"I have not!" Emn nearly yelled.

Nicholas cleared his throat and cocked his head. "Liar."

"I haven't! I've...read the next two in the series. Atalant has them in a digital format on one of her biofilms. She left them up one night after going to bed, and I couldn't sleep, so...yeah. But she doesn't have this one. I don't know why."

Nicholas laughed hard enough that he had to cover his mouth. Tears formed in the corners of his eyes. "Oh my god, she probably got them from a Terran library when she and Yorden visited Mars. This is perfect." He pointed to the book. "Go back to the inn. When she comes in to change for her thing with Arik, offer her a glass of whiskey. Ask her if you can share a page from a new book you found." Nicholas swallowed another round of laughter.

"Read her something from this book. I bet you twenty diamond rounds she's yours for the rest of the night."

"What if I can't get her to sit still long enough to listen to a page or two?"

Nicholas took her hand, waved to the shop assistant, and pulled Emn out into the street. "Don't worry—it'll work. Let's head back, and I'll help you set up. I know that book by heart. There's a sex scene in there I know Atalant won't be able to walk away from. And if you think she might, well, we could go back for some of those handcuffs..."

Emn swatted his shoulder with the paperback, but she was grinning and practically bouncing as they made their way to the ground transport they'd borrowed. She hadn't bothered to pick up her gloves from the first store, and her flightsuit was still zipped down to her collar. No one stared or pointed, and as Nicholas watched Emn climb into the transport, alternately biting her lower lip and smiling to herself, he saw the Emn that had so captivated Atalant on the *Lucidity*. That look would stop Atalant in her tracks, Nicholas was sure, even if the whiskey and book didn't.

Grinning wildly, Nicholas took his seat, fastened his lap and shoulder belts, and closed his eyes. For the very first time in almost a year, Nicholas realized that both he and Emn were truly, genuinely happy. And maybe, just maybe, soon Atalant would be, too.

Legacy

2062 CE

Emn tore herself from the heavy blanket. The room was dark, and she could hear Atalant's steady breathing, but behind all that was the screaming.

It had started as a whine—the sort of high-pitched kind made by engines—and at first, Emn had simply rolled over and assumed the *Scarlet Lucidity* was malfunctioning, but the sound had continued. This wasn't the first time she'd heard it since yesterday, but it was definitely the *loudest*. And this morning...this morning, the pitch had kept increasing until the whine became a lilt. It came in gasps, in segments short enough to be breaths. Just behind it, Emn could hear wracking sobs.

Emn tried to follow the sound, but it was omnipresent...and foreign. Was it telepathic? Maybe? Except, she knew what telepathy felt like, and she knew what Ardulans and Neek felt like, and this voice belonged to neither of those. It was...lengthy. Ardulan voices were more rounded and succinct. Neek voices were also round, but shaped more like an oval—at least, that was how Emn visualized it. All telepathic messages echoed in the same place inside her skull, sort of lower and rightward, near her neck. This voice did too, but it was just...it sounded so *alien.*

Emn shivered. Neither she nor Atalant was clothed, and the room temperature was set to be compatible with the thick blanket that Atalant so enjoyed. Emn could have done without the cooled room, but Atalant tended to stay much closer to Emn in the bed if she was cold, and *that* Emn appreciated.

The whine came again. It was lower this time, more mournful than frightened. Emn stood from the bed, moved to the small porthole—which was barely wider than her hand—and pressed her nose against it. They were docked on Sava, Craston's first moon, in Yorden's private berth. Outside, all she could see was darkness cut through near the floor by yellow track lighting. The sound remained though, made more of sobs now than cries. It didn't seem any louder at the tiny window, so Emn moved to the door. Still the same.

"I'm losing my mind," Emn muttered to herself as she rubbed goosebumps from her arms. Was it a small animal, maybe? A small, creepy animal that Atalant couldn't hear? Emn snorted at her own ridiculousness. Still, Emn walked cautiously back to the bed, knelt down, pushed the bed skirt aside, and peered into yet more darkness, searching, hoping, to find the owner of the sobs.

Nothing was there. Nothing was ever there, but the sound came again, and this time, it was no sad wail, but an excruciating shriek.

"Agh!" Emn clapped her hands over her ears and fell back onto the thick woolen carpet. The scream continued—threatening to shatter her eardrums—for another two heartbeats and then cut off as quickly as it had come.

"Emn?" Atalant's voice was heavy with sleep. Emn only just heard it through her hands. "Emn?" Atalant tried again.

Emn tentatively moved her hands from her head and then shifted back to her knees. Maybe it was just a dream— a lucid dream—and Atalant had just woken her from it. That was...possible, right? That, all those other times, she'd been dreaming too?

"I'm down here." Emn heard Atalant scoot to the edge of the bed, and the sight of Atalant's face peering over the edge of the andal bedframe helped Emn slow her breathing. Atalant had always had that effect on her, even when she was first *don*. Atalant was always so stable, it seemed to Emn—even now. Even after being thrust into a leadership role in a religion she loathed. Even in the early morning when her girlfriend was clearly acting strange.

"Emn? Sweetheart, why are you under the bed? What time is it?"

"It's early, and I...thought I dropped something." Emn stood and slid back under the blanket. She wrapped an arm around Atalant's waist, hoping she could pull the other woman close and go back to sleep, but Atalant pushed herself up on an elbow.

"What did you drop?"

"Hmm?" Emn buried her face in her pillow, willing the screams to stay away. This was the third time she'd heard them. They'd started just as the *Lucidity* entered the Charted Systems, and Emn was more than ready for them to stop.

"You said you dropped something. Did you want me to help look? What are we looking for? Did you bring a biofilm to bed?"

"Nothing. It's nothing. I think I was dreaming, or maybe hearing some stray andal through you." *And I want to have fun on this trip, not end up in a medical facility for hearing voices*, Emn thought darkly to herself.

"Hey." Atalant brushed a lock of dark-red hair from the side of Emn's face and kissed her cheek. "This is supposed to be a vacation, remember? No sentient planets, no whispering trees, and no council meetings." Atalant brushed her hand across Emn's shoulder and down her arm before she slipped it down to Emn's hip. Her fingers began to stroke in small circles at the tight skin there. "Just you and me, Yorden, Nicholas, and Salice on a galactic joyride. No robes. No complications."

The blanket had fallen off Atalant's shoulders and pooled around her waist, exposing the chain of linked hexagons—her Talent marking for Aggression—across her right side. "Even after so long, I'm still not used to these," Emn said, nodding at them. She wanted to trace the raised, black veins that pushed from Atalant's skin, but it seemed silly to do so. Emn knew what they felt like. Her whole body was covered with the same markings that she alternately despised and loved. Despised because they made her an outcast amongst her own people, but loved because they had brought her and Atalant together.

Atalant raised an eyebrow. "You're changing the subject."

"Would you come closer?"

Atalant blinked in surprise, but scooted into Emn's arms. Emn moved to her back as Atalant pillowed her head on top of Emn's breasts and threaded their legs together. Within the heat of her skin against Atalant's, Emn tried to let the last of the scream slip from her mind.

"You're having a hard time with this winding down thing," Atalant remarked. "It's been a year nearly to the day since we left Neek. The damn Ardulan Eld ceremonies are finally over. The Risalians have the Charted Systems back in working order, more or less, and the Mmnnuggls are quiet. We've got Ardulum in a nice, quiet, uninhabited solar system where it can't do any major harm. Now, we all just need to decompress." Atalant looked up and smirked. "I could help you, if you wanted."

Emn smiled and tangled a hand into Atalant's hair. It was loose—a rare occurrence—and the strands were thick and slightly curled.

"I would like that a lot," she responded, glad to have left the conversation about why she was out of bed in the first place. "But I want to take my time because things were very one-sided last night."

Atalant snorted. "My head was comfortable between your legs. I didn't see any point in moving."

"Mmm-hmm. My point is, I don't want to get interrupted halfway through." *And you're going to stay put this time,* she added across their telepathic link.

You could ask the andal to pin me to the bed, I suppose, Atalant suggested with a smirk. *Or cellulose-voodoo the cotton in the bedsheets into a sort of restraint...*

Atalant sent images along with the words, making Emn flush. "I'll be certain to bring a potted andal tree along next time. But right now"—Emn glanced at the digits glowing on the wall—"we've about an hour before we promised we'd meet the others. Time for breakfast?"

A heavy sigh came from Atalant as she nuzzled Emn's neck. "I have some andal in the captain's quarters. I can reach it from here. You wouldn't even have to leave the bed."

"And when your stomach starts growling?" Emn asked. "You're going to eat andal too?"

Atalant pushed herself up and looked at Emn with a long, deliberate stare while her right hand trailed down Emn's stomach and gently cupped her between the legs.

"Atalant," Emn said reproachfully, although the warmth of Atalant's hand caused her hips to rise involuntarily from the bed.

"If you insist. You know, nothing says we have to leave the ship on this vacation. The rest could go take a lengthy shore leave, and we could explore the various nooks and crannies"—Emn opened her mouth, but Atalant jumped back in—"of the *Lucidity*, although I'm open to other suggestions."

This time, Emn giggled. The screaming seemed more like a distant memory now, fading as fast as a dream. Maybe she was just tired and worn down from the last year and a half or so. Whatever it was that was causing the noise, it could wait. She and Atalant had done enough waiting for a lifetime.

Emn squirmed out from under Atalant, put her hands on her own hips, and tilted her head. Atalant's eyes were looking everywhere but at her face, so Emn grabbed a green shirt from the floor and tossed it onto the bed. Atalant wrinkled her nose in response.

"Breakfast first," Emn ordered as she grabbed another shirt and pulled it over her head. "With clothes. Then, we can talk about whether we're leaving this ship at all in the next two weeks."

* * *

"Where's Atalant?" Nicholas asked as he all but skipped into the galley of the *Lucidity*, where Emn was finishing off a steamed andal twig. He was dressed smartly in fitted brown pants that ended just above his ankles and a pale-blue collared shirt. His thick, black hair was neatly braided, and he walked with the confidence of an adult, although there was no hiding the youthfulness of his steps. Emn sat back in the thick cushioning of the chair and smiled. It was good to see Nicholas out of his flightsuit and out of Ardulan work clothes. He was home—well, closer to home than he'd been in a long time—and Emn envied the lightness he carried even after everything.

"She's just gone to change her shirt," Emn responded. She finished off her piece of andal and sipped water from a plastic cup.

Nicholas chuckled as he tore off a piece of bread from a loaf they'd brought from Ardulum and flopped into the nearest chair. "And what happened to her old one?"

Emn looked at him wryly. "She spilled juice on it. Nothing else."

"Uh-huh."

"Don't you have a meeting to prepare for?"

Nicholas swallowed the bread and dusted his hands over the tabletop. "Yeah, but I can't go anywhere without Yorden and Atalant. It's great that the notary was willing to meet us in the Alusian System, but only Yorden can certify my Journey completion certificate, and since we're on Atalant's ship now, she has to be the one to sign me on for apprenticeship. I'm still too young to officially be on my own, at least by Charted Systems standards, so thank god Mom was willing to go for the apprentice extension, especially after I managed to get involved in two separate wars."

Yorden entered the galley, grunted at both of them, and headed to the corner where the oldest piece of technology Emn had ever seen, a Terran coffee pot, sat against the wall. It was held together with biofilm plaster and funny-looking silver tape and smelled like moldy perf.

"Good morning, Cap— Yorden." Emn still slipped on the honorific, especially when they were all onboard a ship. Fortunately, the slip brought a smile to Yorden's face, which was rare before he'd had at least two cups of coffee.

"And just where is that girlfriend of yours?" Yorden asked as the coffee began to percolate.

Nicholas answered before Emn could. "Getting dressed. Again. But the better question is, where's *yours*, Yorden?"

Yorden cleared his throat for what felt like an excessively long time before answering. "Salice has had too many early mornings throughout her life and has been quite firm about not getting out of bed until she is damn well ready. This morning, that may not be until lunch." He turned and winked at Emn. "Atalant, on the other hand, was always an early riser."

"Atalant spilled *bilaris* fruit juice on her shirt because the damn pitcher handle broke off and doesn't appreciate your insinuation," Atalant said as she stalked back into the galley, took a swipe at Yorden's arm, which he deftly avoided, and sat down heavily in the chair to Emn's left.

"You had no other clean shirts?" Nicholas raised his eyebrows and gestured at the knee-length, pale-blue dress that Atalant wore along with some mid-calf utility boots. "We've been off Ardulum for, like, fifteen hours, and most of those, in theory, we've all been asleep."

Recognizing Atalant's souring mood, Emn stood and put a hand on Atalant's shoulder, dipping her fingers ever so slightly under the scooped neckline. "Nicholas," Emn said in a low voice, "do you have any idea how hard it was to get her to even print this?"

Atalant folded her arms across her chest, which only succeeded in buoying her breasts, and frowned. "I'm allowed to wear dresses, people. You're all allowed to wear dresses. They're comfortable and let *stuk* evaporate properly, and for the first time in forever, I'm not stuck at a console or table for twelve hours straight. Leave it be."

Emn expected at least a smirk from Nicholas, but the young man smiled instead. "You look pretty, Atalant."

"Yeah, yeah. Let's go get your paperwork done." Atalant covered Emn's hand with her own and squeezed it. "You'll come too, right?" she asked, looking up at Emn. "Should only take an hour or so, and after that, we're on our own."

"We should meet for dinner," Yorden interjected as he finished the black sludge in his cup. "First day of vacation drinking. Salice should be awake by then."

Emn's stomach dropped a little—not because she didn't want to spend time with the crew, but because she *did* have every intention of taking revenge on Atalant for last night's rather one-sided lovemaking. That wasn't going to happen if they were all drunk.

You'll still have me for lunch, Atalant reminded her after Emn's thoughts leaked across their telepathic bond. *I promise to behave.*

That brightened Emn considerably. She offered Atalant a hand up, being sure to take in the flow of the dress around Atalant's thick legs and wide hips as she stood. *I suppose that—*

The scream came again, worse than ever. It scraped the back of her skull and wound through her ears, the sound of an animal caught in a snare. A screech of desperation and fear. Emn fell to her side and screamed back into the void. She clawed at her ears, at the back of her head, yelling to drown out the screaming and the pain.

Emn! Atalant's voice edged through the wall of noise, but Emn couldn't form words. She was dying. Her world was dying, and she was watching. She was being forced into a metal cylinder by Risalians. The voice in her head cried out for help, for a mother, and Emn yelled for her own.

EMN!

The screaming stopped as suddenly as it had started. Emn took a moment to breathe, to rest her raw throat, before she opened her eyes.

She was lying on the carpeted floor of the galley, curled in a fetal position. Atalant had a steel grip on her arm and was fumbling to get another under her to lift Emn upright. Yorden and Nicholas were down on the floor too, their faces etched in concern.

"Just a funny dream, I think," Emn said as Atalant eased her into a sitting position. Although Atalant didn't say anything, Emn felt the other woman's *stuk* thin in concern. She tried to force a smile.

"Where I come from, we call those terrors," Yorden said. Emn caught him pass a look to Atalant that she couldn't discern. "This your first one?"

Emn wanted to lie, but with Atalant right there, her *stuk* bleeding all over Emn's wrist, she doubted very much she would get away with it. It didn't seem fair to burden all of them with what was likely just some repressed first-*don* issue that her mind finally had time to process. This was supposed to be a vacation, after all. She didn't want to deal with this. She didn't want to deal with *anything*, outside of how to keep Atalant's clothes on the floor.

"There have been a few others," she admitted.

"How many others?" Atalant's voice had an edge that made Emn shiver. It was her Eld voice, the voice that had taken command of entire worlds and was slipping easily into a role of unarguable leadership.

"A few."

"How many, Emn?"

Emn sighed and slouched. "This is the fourth, but they're not a big deal. They don't usually make me scream like that. Really. I've had nightmares before. A lot, actually, when I was with the Risalians." Of course, these weren't anything like those, but that was irrelevant.

"Christ," Yorden muttered. "For how long now?"

Atalant's grip on her wrist had loosened, but Emn could feel the tension in her body as she leaned against it.

"It's not a big deal." She pushed herself up, but Atalant's hand fell on her shoulder.

"Emn." That was Eld Atalant. Emn shivered.

"Since we left Ardulum. They started the moment we entered the Systems. Well, this particular type, anyway. They're...different from my normal nightmares."

"Why didn't you—"

"They're short. Never longer than a minute, and they're...telepathic. I think. Or a memory of telepathy. Maybe being on Ardulum got me used to people being guarded with their telepathy, and someone out here is just...spraying emotions or something. Please stop worrying over nothing." Emn kissed a very stern-looking Atalant on the cheek.

"If it was telepathic, Emn, I think I would have heard it. I should have the same telepathy potential as you, if not slightly more with the andal stuff."

Emn tucked a lock of hair behind Atalant's ear, hoping she could make the Eld part of Atalant revert to vacation mode. "Yes, but I have a bunch of marks that we don't even understand. Besides, stray telepathy isn't dangerous, just irritating. If it gets worse, I'll see a healer, but until then, could we just forget it? I'm not in any danger. I just need to relax, and Nicholas needs his paperwork."

"We are late," Yorden admitted as he stood. Nicholas followed suit, remaining uncharacteristically quiet. "Atalant?"

"You're *sure* you're okay?"

Emn rolled her shoulders. "I know my limits, Atalant."

After staring at her for an uncomfortable moment, Atalant nodded. "We could revisit this after we get Nicholas's apprenticeship in order."

"Or until after lunch," Emn added hopefully. She allowed Atalant to help her stand and then brushed off the side of her pants. "Waiting another few hours won't make any difference."

* * *

"And you swear by your solemn rights as a Charted Systems citizen that you take this oath freely and without duress, and that you understand the restrictions imposed by your age and station?"

"I do."

Emn watched from the far side of the room as Nicholas signed the biofilm, Yorden standing to his left, Atalant to his right. She couldn't help but grin along with him. In Terran culture, yearly aging seemed to come without any large ceremonies, but in many ways, Emn thought this felt very much like a *don* ceremony. Ardulans kept growing through their first *don* and didn't reach their full height until second *don,* but she remembered standing next to Nicholas, her head just below his shoulder, in the cockpit of the *Pledge.* She remembered their late-night stories and how he could make any number of improper sounds that had Atalant scowling from across a room.

She remembered their stolen Mmnnuggl pod and trying to figure out her new body. Looking at Nicholas now—as he straightened and shook hands with the notary, as Yorden clapped him on the back and Atalant gave him a hug—she remembered how similar they had been. And it was hard not to think about how different things would have been if she had gotten to embark on Youth Journey. Or travel at all. Or been perceived as a sentient being.

The notary, a Risalian with hair just greening at the temples, scanned the document, nodded, folded it, and put it in a wooden briefcase. "The film will be filed tonight and will show up on the record tomorrow." Xe leaned on the edge of an andal desk that spanned the width of the small room and let hir black, curved claws clack irritatingly against it. Of course, the notary was Risalian. Plenty of other species had taken up administrative government roles since the Crippling War, but it was inevitable, wasn't it, that they'd still end up with a Risalian.

"You understand that he cannot begin work until tomorrow," the Risalian finally concluded after staring an uncomfortably long time at Atalant.

"That's fine," Atalant responded. "We're not going anywhere for a bit. Anything else?"

The Risalian's blue eyes flicked to Emn. They'd done that a dozen times already. She wanted to pluck those white orbs from hir head and mash them into a paste between her hands.

"Anything else?" Atalant prompted again.

"No." The notary replied, hesitation gone. Xe held out two long claws toward Nicholas, who tapped them once with his right hand. "Congratulations, Nicholas St. John of Earth. You are hereby signed to the *Scarlet Lucidity* for a period of one year, until such time as you come of age. On your birthday, the contract will be null and void and you will be free to move about the Systems without any form of supervision."

"Great!" Nicholas grinned and, without any warning, ran back to Emn, took her hand, and half pulled her toward the door. "Come on. Enough with this stuff. Let's head out and catch a ferry to Craston proper."

Emn raised an eyebrow. "Nicholas, I was sort of hoping for—"

"*One* hour. That's barely any time at all." He turned back to Emn with a lopsided grin. "I'm not a Journey youth anymore. I'm not some stupid kid anymore. It's like I've..." He searched for the words. "Like I've just come out of my first *don* and am ready to start my life, you know. I want to celebrate with my friends."

Emn's insides melted a little. He was right. This was a time to celebrate with friends. Yorden was a mentor and Atalant was her lover, but Nicholas...Nicholas was her first friend. Her only friend, really, although she and Miketh were making reasonable strides in that direction, and Arik made an attempt to talk to her on a regular basis. There was Salice, too, but Emn had not spent much time with the other Risalian Ardulan since her and Yorden's courtship had blossomed. Nicholas was right. He deserved a celebration, and she needed to be there.

"Of course, Nick. Let me just tell Salice to get up and dressed. By the time we make it back to the *Lucidity*'s berth, she should be ready to go. Where do you want to head first?"

"Well, they have these waterslides on that little continent in the southern hemisphere—"

Anything else Nicholas said was lost as Emn reached out to the place in her head that Salice's consciousness occupied from time to time. *Hey, friend. Ready to get up? We're heading to Craston to celebrate Nicholas's graduation.*

No response.

Salice? Emn asked again, sending her consciousness outward and into the ship. Salice was good at cutting herself off from the thin threads of perpetual telepathy that held most Ardulans together, even if they seldom used them, so Emn focused her efforts. *Salice?*

Emn couldn't find her on the *Lucidity*. She broadened her search to the nearby berths, then to the commerce area, and then, finally, to the entire station. There was nothing. Not a hint of the disordered, sometimes-chaotic mind belonging to Salice.

The screaming started again.

* * *

"She just wasn't there. I don't know what else to tell you." Emn blew hair from her face and slouched into the thick velvet pillow behind her. Salice sat to her left on the same oversized, garish couch in the *Lucidity*'s game room— of course it had a game room—and Atalant was in front of her, sitting far too upright in a bioplastic chair and staring at Emn like she was some strange perf flavor no one had ever tried before.

"But she's here now, right?"

Salice rolled her eyes. Emn threw her hands up in exasperation. "Well, of course she's here now. I'm not suggesting that she stopped existing for a few moments, just that she was...removed from the telepathic network for a short time. Or something was blocking her. Or overriding her. I don't know."

Atalant frowned. "Like what Corccinth did to me when we first arrived on Ardulum?"

"Sort of. Yeah, I suppose it was a lot like that. But I guess maybe I could have been the one removed from the network, although I don't think you went missing at all, Atalant."

"But would I?" Atalant pursed her lips. "Our connection has twin backups. I can hear you through a *stuk* connection, and we haven't gone more than five minutes without touching one another since we arrived. We're connected by the andal too, which does not require telepathy as we understand it. So, I'm not sure we can judge your telepathy through our own connection."

"And I guess there is no shortage of people who'd want to mess with Emn," Yorden noted as he entered the room, Nicholas trailing behind. They both looked grimy, and Emn wrinkled her nose at the smell of Terran sweat. Salice waved a hand in front of her face.

"Ugh, why, you two?" Atalant asked. She stood and backed farther away from the two men.

"Because football is fun and there is an excellent sports arena here," Yorden answered. "I'd have invited you, but I assumed you and Emn had other strenuous exercise planned, and Salice has made her opinion on contact sports very clear. She also decided against getting her vocal cords repaired, if any of you are curious why she's not talking after yesterday's consult. She didn't want to elaborate, but if she's happy, I'm happy. Her body and all."

Salice blew a raspberry at Yorden. He chuckled in response, but when he went to sit next to her, she shook her head and pointed to the door. Nicholas laughed.

"Seriously? It's sweat. I'm a mammal."

Salice's finger stayed erect.

"Am I at least allowed to stand in the corner?"

Salice released a *put-put* sound.

"Fine." Yorden clasped Nicholas on the shoulder, and the two walked to the far side of the room. "To the more pressing matter—"

"Says you." Nicholas turned his head. "We're right over the forced air. We *do* smell bad." He tugged on Yorden's shirt. "Shower. Junior officer mandate."

Yorden rolled his eyes but followed Nicholas out into the hall. That left Atalant staring at Emn with another one of her Eld looks.

Emn cringed. "I'm not broken! Everything's fine right now. When the screaming comes, I can still feel everything

I'm supposed to. It's not...it's not like part of my mind is being shut down. It feels more like...like something is being superimposed."

"We never said you were! Emn, I'm sorry," Atalant said, face stricken. "So, it's...just like telepathy, but telepathy that neither Salice nor I can hear, despite being genetically nearly identical to you?"

Emn did *not* like where this line of thinking would lead. "Atalant—"

Why?

Salice's mental voice startled both Emn and Atalant. Salice so rarely communicated with words—preferring mental images or simple hand gestures—that for a moment, Emn wasn't certain how to respond.

"I suppose that is the big question, isn't it? Emn?" Atalant raised an eyebrow as her voice became far too formal. "Can you offer any suggestions about this or Salice's 'disappearance'?"

Emn tilted her head and frowned at Atalant. "Eld Atalant, if you're insinuating that the screaming in my head is also related to Salice's absence, or that this is all just in my head and not some rogue telepathy, then why don't we take the *Lucidity* back to Ardulum and get me to a healer?"

Atalant sat back, visibly stung. Emn almost apologized for using Atalant's title, but then thought better of it. Atalant had grown marvelously into her leadership role on Ardulum, but it meant that sometimes that unconscious authority seeped into their personal lives, too.

Atalant rubbed her temples. "I'm sorry, sweetheart. I'm just trying to understand. Salice, like every Ardulan I know, is a constant buzzing in my head, along with about a billion andal trees. She's always there. Vacation or not, we may have to turn back."

I was sleeping when you tried to find me. Salice patted Emn's knee, seemingly oblivious to the tension between the other two women. *Perhaps I was deeply dreaming.*

"That doesn't remove you from our collective consciousness though," Atalant said after a moment. "It just makes you harder to reach. And reach, for Emn, has never been a problem."

"Well, maybe I *am* broken. Batteries only last so long, after all." Emn stood and marched to the other side of the room. She took her steps a little too quickly and bashed her hip against the edge of a standing game board—some Keft strategy game none of them could figure out how to play.

"Fuck!"

"Hey." Atalant slid in next to her, deftly avoiding the offending table. She put her hand over Emn's, which was rubbing the soon-to-be bruise, and put her other hand on Emn's shoulder. *I don't mean to be a* titha, Atalant sent privately. *I'm sorry. I just want us all to be able to relax and enjoy these two weeks. Whatever you want to do, whether it's go back to Ardulum or stay here and hope things get better, I'm behind you.*

Emn let her head loll back to stare at the textured ceiling. The attention to ridiculous detail on the *Lucidity*, a relic of its original owner, made the entire situation feel comical. "Do you think there's something wrong with me, Atalant?"

"No." Atalant's answer was much more emphatic than Emn had expected. When Atalant didn't continue and the silence stretched too long, Emn sighed and put her head on Atalant's shoulder.

"But you still think I should see a healer."

"Yes. No. Emn..." Atalant tangled a hand into Emn's hair and pulled her into an embrace. "Maybe we should just tighten our link for a while. If I can hear it, too...I don't know. Maybe it'll be something I recognize."

"Mm." Emn kissed Atalant's ear. Salice chortled. "And we're supposed to be able to focus on everyone else how, with this open connection?"

"You were the one who suggested not leaving the ship for two weeks."

"Yes, but Atalant, we have to eat, surely."

That same pointed state returned to Atalant's face. All Emn could think was that if her species still produced *stuk*, she'd be standing in a puddle of it right then. "That wasn't what I meant."

Atalant smirked.

* * *

Emn traced the annual rings on the wooden bar top while sipping a fizzy juice whose name she couldn't pronounce. Although she was wearing thin cotton pants and a short-sleeved shirt, she was pleasantly warm. Whether this was from the juice or because she and Atalant had done everything *except* sleep last night, Emn wasn't sure. Atalant was soaking in the *Lucidity*'s giant jet bath now—alone, by request, so she could actually get clean—so Emn had wandered to the nearest bar. Said bar, called *Divorce Settlement II,* was clean and well lit, and with Yorden and Nicholas playing a Terran game with balls and sticks on a table in the far corner, it felt downright comfortable. It smelled like Yorden's coffee, which Emn did not care for, but the juice was good, and the bartender didn't try to make small talk.

"Would it be all right if I sat here?"

Emn swiveled on her chair to face...an Ardulan? She sucked in a deep breath and scanned the person's exposed skin. Dark circles under the eyes. No Talent markings, but they had five fingers per hand, short and orange hair that curled in waves across their forehead, and pale skin—maybe not *translucently* pale, but it was hard to tell. However, there were a number of markings that could easily be covered by clothes. Curious, Emn mentally prodded the being, but there was no response. Not telepathic, then, or perhaps they had it blocked off. Emn was certainly capable of doing that, but she didn't make a habit of it. Still, maybe a human?

"Uh, yes. Yes, of course." Though, there were plenty of other stools at the bar, with no one else sitting on them. Emn's stomach fluttered as she connected the dots. "Uh—"

"I'm August. I saw you looked a little confused. I'm Terran, and I fall into one of the minor gender categories. Nonbinary—and transmasculine, if you want to get technical about it."

Emn blushed in embarrassment. "It wasn't about that, really."

August smiled brightly. Their cheeks dimpled, accentuating the smattering of freckles on their face that Emn had been too busy searching for Talent markings to notice before. "It's all right. I'd be more upset if you were a Terran, but it's clear you're not. Where are you from? Your skin has an unusual opacity."

That was one way to put it, Emn supposed. She had never actually been picked up in a bar before and had no idea how to respond. "I'm, uh—"

"My girlfriend." Atalant came up beside her and slid two very suggestive fingers across Emn's shoulders. With their connection so strong, it was impossible for Emn not to react, and the images her mind conjured—of Atalant flushed on their bed, of the way their mouths fit together—buoyed into Atalant's mind and sent her *stuk* production into overdrive. Stickiness bled through Emn's shirt and dribbled down her back, which helped cool her down.

"Oh!" August's smile faltered as they took in Atalant's appearance. "You're... Of course. Excuse me, I didn't realize." They stood from the bench, turned, and then looked back over their shoulder. "Still, lot of redheads here today. It's kind of fun. Since I'm supremely excellent at awkward flirting, I'll probably see you two around again." They grabbed a short glass of amber liquid from the bar and, much to Emn's amazement, downed it in one gulp.

Emn giggled, and even Atalant let out a chortle. "See you around, then," Emn said and waved as August moved to a bench near the door.

"Cute gatoi," Atalant said coyly as she sat on the vacated chair. "Looking to branch out?"

"They weren't gatoi, I don't think. Nicholas told me once that there are way more than three genders on Earth.

Anyway, I never thought you'd be jealous, Atalant." Emn took Atalant's hand in her own and kissed the top. "Especially after last night."

Atalant's smile faded. She stroked a thumb over Emn's knuckles and looked over at Yorden and Nicholas, who were whooping over the sports game feed streaming on a wall-mounted biofilm. "I think, for a moment, I thought they were Ardulan. Maybe it's silly to think about this now, but when we're out here in the Systems, do you miss Ardulum? Miss Ardulans? I...realize we've never really talked about bringing a gatoi into the relationship, never thought to ask if you'd ever want to. *Is* that something you'd want?"

"Atalant, I barely have time to sleep with you. I don't need a third person's schedule to keep track of. And I can miss my people without wanting to sleep with the first one I meet. Besides, *you're* my people. Or, did you forget already?"

A smile played at the corners of Atalant's mouth. "No, love, I didn't forget. The andal won't let me forget."

Emn leaned in and kissed her, lingering on still-swollen lips until she heard Yorden's voice shout, "You two have a whole damn ship!" from across the bar. Grinning, Emn took Atalant's hand and led her to the door, past August who winked conspiratorially at them, and into the corridor that led to the docking area. Seeing the redheaded Terran again pushed Emn's thoughts away from Atalant and the *Lucidity* and toward a thought she'd often pondered, but never vocalized.

Do you ever think about them? she asked over their link, not wanting to speak lest the words sound silly. *The other subspecies, like the Keft? Or even other sold flares? The Risalians can't have been the only ones to score that deal. Would we recognize them, do you think, if we saw them? What if they weren't telepathic? How would I tell a subspecies from a redheaded Terran and a Keft who didn't have claws due to a genetic mutation?*

Atalant paused as they neared the boarding ramp to the *Lucidity* and turned to face Emn. The smell of disinfectant and recycled air was stronger here than anywhere else on the station, and it stung Emn's nose and made her eyes water.

"I don't think the genetics work like that, Emn. Arik has been working with me on that, and Corccinth has done some fascinating research over the years. Telepathy is our common denominator, outside of being bipedal. There are other telepathic species, of course—and thousands, if not millions, of bipedal ones—but only those with telepathy can access telekinesis, on any level, and all the known species capable of *that* have some sort of relationship to *stuk* and variants on the genes that cause red hair. It's a pretty unique set of traits, all put together. I don't think anyone with them would just be wandering about." Her voice dropped an octave as she put a hand on Emn's shoulder. "What about the screaming? Have you heard it today yet?"

"No, not today." Emn managed a smile. "Stop worrying, love. I'm okay. I'm sure it's just stress."

"Salice?" Atalant prodded. "Can you reach her?"

Emn fought the urge to roll her eyes. She reached out into the *Lucidity* and scanned the various rooms. Salice wasn't in the room she shared with Yorden, but it was nearing dinnertime. Emn checked the galley next and then the cockpit. When she still couldn't find the other Ardulan, she broadened her reach to the docking bay, the bar, and then across the station.

Salice? Emn broadcasted as loudly as she could, knowing Atalant would overhear. She tried to banish the panic churning in her stomach and pushed the call not just outward, but into her head, thinking it might better boost the signal. *SALICE!*

Who is Salice?

Emn's breath caught. The voice was slow and lingered on the back of her neck like the sludge Yorden poured from the bottom of his coffee pot. It felt detached and had a surreal dream-like quality. Except, Emn was awake. Atalant was still staring at her expectantly, probably waiting for Emn to admit she couldn't find Salice, that something was broken in her head, that this vacation had been doomed from the start and they all needed to pick up and go back to Ardulum so Emn could see a healer.

Atalant? Emn tried to aim the thought, keeping it private. She could still feel Atalant—her presence was a persistent, thin reed that fluttered in the back of Emn's head—but her call rebounded to the back of Emn's brain, following some neural pathway Emn didn't recognize.

Atalant? the voice repeated, pondering. It didn't seem to care for a response. And the being sounded...drunk? Well, maybe not drunk, but definitely tipsy.

"Atalant?" Emn said out loud. Her voice echoed oddly, and Atalant's response, when it came, was like a bell sounding underwater.

"What's wrong, Emn? She answered your call. I heard her. Can you not?"

Emn swallowed. She couldn't hear anything right now, in fact, other than Atalant's muted voice. The background din of the spaceport had dropped away. There was a swishing in her ears, the sound of low, shallow breathing, and a heartbeat—not hers. "Something's wrong."

Atalant's brow furrowed. "Let's get on the ship. We're going to call Corccinth and a healer and see if they can diagnose from there or if we have to go back. Come on." She offered Emn her hand, but Emn didn't take it. Her limbs felt heavy, her breathing depressed.

"Atalant," she began, her lips barely moving, "I think I'm in a lucid dream. Rather, I think I'm sharing someone else's dream. Or maybe their hallucination."

Atalant said something in response, but her voice dropped away. Emn's vision, too, grayed, before darkening. She blinked furiously, still too heavy to bring up her hands to rub at her eyes, when the voice came again.

I didn't think I was this drunk, but I've never had 'bourbon' before. Are you supposed to be here?

I don't know. Who are you?

The voice paused, and confusion filtered into Emn's head. *This is my nightmare. Who are YOU?*

Nightmare?

The warm sleepiness of Emn's mind was whisked away, and sharp fear replaced it. The darkness bled into an agricultural scene, the sunset blood red, the fields flat and golden. Emn looked down to see her bare feet buried in dried husks of some plant material. The dirt felt dry under her feet, and the sun was too warm. There was no breeze. The hot air burned her lungs as she sucked in deep breaths. She heard no animal calls or insect hums. There was only the sun beating down on her, the ground leaching her sweat, and the dead fields that spanned past the horizon.

There used to be a library here, the voice said. *And around it, andal plantations as far as you could see. I've seen the pictures. We have a recreation of the library on the system's fifth planet.*

Emn's patience wore out. *But what planet is this?*

Here it comes, the voice said. A hand brushed the back of her own, and the alien presence seemed to fill up her mind. Emn felt shorter. She was sweating, the leather clothes she had on suddenly too restrictive, the hat on her head stifling. When she looked down, she realized she was in tight pants and her arms were free of markings. She looked up at the sun. Sweat or *stuk*—Emn couldn't tell— beaded on her face, even under her oxygen mask, and the thick leathers she wore were stained dark. The hair on her shoulder was red—blood red, sun red—her skin the same golden brown as the desiccated stalks that covered Emn's feet. Realization bubbled into Emn's thoughts. She checked her hands. Five fingers per hand, each tipped with a delicate blue feather peppered with downy barbs.

Look, the voice said. The sound was flat, but underneath it, Emn felt the growing terror. Wind caught her hair and blew it into her eyes. The smell of salt stung her nose as bits of dirt powdered against her ear. Larger pieces of the ground spun around her. The soil under her feet shifted.

She heard a terrible cracking, then a popping, and then the sound of a world being sliced at its seams. There was no andal to scream, but there was no need. The voice screamed. Emn screamed.

A long, rounded shadow fell across her, but Emn didn't need to look up to know what was looming in the sky, what monstrosity had visited this planet and traumatized its people, destroyed its ecosystems, and mutated its weather and tides. The air shook. When the ground gave way, Emn let herself be devoured.

* * *

The first thing Emn felt when she awoke was the rawness of her throat. The second thing was the soft feeling of cloth-covered breasts against her cheek, and the third was the weight of one of Atalant's legs threaded over hers. She didn't trust her eyes yet, so she slid her hand to Atalant's hip and gripped the rounded bone there. Atalant's even breathing turned erratic, but she didn't stir, so Emn edged her hand over and cupped Atalant's backside. The dream, the connection, the whatever it was, felt far away now and was slipping from her mind in sheets. What had seemed so terrifying that she'd screamed her throat raw now felt like a lingering chill that she could smother with Atalant's mouth. Emn opened her eyes to an unmade bed, artificial sunlight creeping up the unpainted wall of their room, and Atalant staring groggily down at her.

Emn stroked the flesh under her hand, traveling down to cup the junction where bottom met thigh and then back up over the hip and around again. Atalant wasn't wearing pants, but she was wearing underwear, and that was unfortunate.

"This was not how I expected this morning to start." Atalant's voice sounded as raw as Emn's throat felt. Emn pursed her lips and reluctantly dragged her head from its perfect pillow.

"Are you lodging a complaint against my hand?"

Atalant croaked a laugh. "No, but maybe I could have some explanation first. You screamed for an hour, Emn! You finally stopped when I dragged you to bed and you buried yourself, well—" Atalant gestured to her breasts.

Emn tried to shrug nonchalantly. "They're comfortable. Familiar." Still, Emn felt that, despite all their time together, she had not had sufficient time to explore how the slope from shoulder to breast melted seamlessly into dark areolas and pert nipples, how a short breath of air raised numerous points of sensitivity, how—when she cupped each—she had to work to contain them. Atalant's breasts captivated Emn. Apparently, they captivated her enough to shake her loose from the shared dream, and now that it had blurred almost to nothing, Emn was grateful for the reprieve.

"Do you remember anything?" Atalant sat up, which brought in a rush of cool air as the blanket slid from their bodies. Emn shivered and sat up as well, but no matter how much she tried to chase the dream, she could mostly just remember feelings.

"I remember being afraid. I remember...heat. I remember panic. Maybe some red hair. There might have been red hair curling in front of my eyes."

"An Ardulan?" Atalant asked, her voice unusually high.

"This was..." Emn raked her mind for memory fragments. "This voice belonged to someone...a gatoi? Not Ardulan though. Not Neek. There were...there were feathers. Maybe quills?" Emn rubbed at her forehead. Feathers seemed ridiculous. Surely her mind had made that part up.

"A subspecies? There are hundreds, you know. Ardulum has been traveling for a long, long time. Those tapestries that we, ah, eventually hung"—Atalant cleared her throat—"they don't go back through Ardulum's entire history. Your telepathic reach, Emn, is farther than even Ardulum's, I'm willing to bet. You might have been right. This might be a genetic cousin you're connecting to."

"If I am, shouldn't you be able to hear them, too?"

Atalant ran her fingers through a mess of tangles near the base of her skull. Her brow wrinkled. "Maybe? Maybe not. I'm not Ardulan, Emn, much as the andal tries. Without the andal's help, my telepathy isn't as good as an Ardulan's and certainly nowhere near yours. I hear what the andal hears, and not all subspecies can hear the andal. The Keft can't. I'm sure there are others."

"So, what do we *do*?" Emn grabbed a handful of the blanket and threw it from the bed. "I'm officially grumpy."

"I vote we call Corccinth. She knows Ardulan history better than anyone. But first, we have a nice, leisurely breakfast and bring everyone else up to speed. Your concert yesterday unnerved even Yorden, so I think some reassurances are in order. I know I feel a lot lighter thinking about this as an issue in interstellar communication, instead of..."

"Instead of something going wrong with me, since the only ones who would know how to fix it would be Cell-Tal." Emn could hear the bitterness dripping from her words.

Atalant puffed out her cheeks and slowly exhaled. "Don't melt me, but it might be a good idea to reach out to them. I don't think there is anything wrong with you, but... Yes, we need information—but don't you also need, I don't know, closure?"

Emn could only glare. There were plenty of words she wanted to use. Picking only a few choice ones was difficult.

"Cell-Tal has your information," Atalant continued softly. "We don't know anything about your genetics, Emn. If we have a wayward caller, understanding your telepathy may help us find them. But even if not, I think you...you probably just need to talk to the Risalians. What they did to you was horrible, but they're diverse and the most irritating ones are all dead. You can't go through your whole life hating every one you come across."

"I hate everything you just said."

Atalant nodded and patted the area next to her. "I know. But you're not arguing, and I appreciate that. Reward? Apology?" She lifted her thin shirt—the one that hugged her hips and waist so well that Emn had often tried to convince her to wear it during the day—over her head and let it fall to the floor. She wore nothing underneath.

Emn's breath caught. "You may have to apologize for a while," she said as she pushed Atalant back down onto the mattress. "Also, we may miss breakfast."

* * *

They emerged into the galley a few hours later, washed, dressed, and ravenous. Yorden, Nicholas, and Salice were already there, sitting at a round table with a deck of playing cards. Nicholas hunched over his hand and interrogated his cards while Salice looked amused and unconcerned with the entire ordeal. Yorden... Emn could tell when he looked up to greet them that he hadn't slept well. His hair was unbrushed, which he'd gotten a lot better about since Salice had come aboard, and there were dark circles under his eyes. An empty mug sat to his left, a deep-brown stain on the inside.

Atalant broke from Emn, keyed in the code for her favorite breakfast into the food printer, and then leaned against a bulkhead while it printed. "Did you actually take Salice to see the Minoran cabaret last night?" she asked incredulously.

Nicholas placed his cards into a neat pile on the table and turned to look at Atalant. "They did. I left after an hour. Much like horses on Earth, the Minorans are...endowed, and there is a *lot* of flapping. Also, the alcohol was way too strong. I could hardly see after the first one."

Salice's laughter tinkled through Emn's head. It was followed by an image of Nicholas laughing far too loudly as he tried on a Minoran bell skirt, his orange drink only a quarter of the way gone. Emn sucked her lips in, trying to stifle a smile.

"We're still on for today though? Unless...healer?" Nicholas looked from Atalant to Emn and then at Yorden. "We're going to get an explanation, right?"

Yorden sat back in his chair and folded his arms across his chest. "That's why I'm still here, anyway. Quite a show you put on for us yesterday, Emn. What is going on?"

Emn looked at Atalant, who shrugged and took a large bite of bacon. *Please brush your teeth before you kiss me*, Emn sent. Atalant winked.

"We think...we think I'm picking up some telepathy, or a version of telepathy, from another subspecies. Unfortunately, the connection isn't stable enough for me to really communicate, and the images slip from me like dreams when I pull out of them."

Yorden set his cards down and stared at Emn with a very disconcerting paternal look that made Emn feel like a first *don* again. "Are we going back or forward, then?" he asked.

"What?"

Salice pushed an image of Corccinth to Emn, followed by an image of a generic Risalian colored with distaste.

Emn frowned while Yorden continued, apparently unaware that Salice had already explained. "Are we going to head back to Ardulum so Corccinth can sort it out, or are we going to go to Risal and let Cell-Tal poke around?" He took a sip from his mug, tapping the bottom when no liquid readily appeared. "I assume Corccinth is preferred, but I can't imagine Atalant didn't argue that the Risalians would likely have answers."

"I am *not* going to Risal!" Emn stalked toward the door, fuming.

Salice sent another image of herself looming over a gray-clad Risalian as xe ran a dermal scanner over Emn. She could feel the other Ardulan's disgust at the thought of the Risalians, but behind it was worry, and that was harder to ignore. Especially coming from Salice.

"I thought this was supposed to be a vacation," Emn muttered at the ground.

"If we get this sorted quickly—say, maybe by inviting a Cell-Tal engineer to meet us tomorrow to do a quick once-over—it still can be." Yorden walked to Emn and put a beefy hand on her shoulder. "I burned a planet to save Atalant, and I *like* the Neek people. Don't think I wouldn't do the same for you, Emn."

Emn managed a small smile. Yorden's words helped the twisting, sick feeling she got when thinking about anything involving Risal, but nothing would ever get rid of the underlying anxiety. Atalant was the same any time they talked about her homeworld, so it wasn't that Emn didn't *understand* her own emotions. They were rational. She had every right to be angry. She just...hated that the Risalians knew so much about her. That information, her genetics, was *hers*. That it was likely stored in some Cell-Tal database, accessible to any Risalian inquiry? That was infuriating.

Never alone, Atalant sent. She slid up next to Emn and wrapped an arm around her waist. Emn let go of a sigh and curled into Atalant's arms.

"You say that, but we'll end up surrounded by Mmnnuggls, or sentient fungi, or it'll turn out Ardulum has a twin world somewhere. Our history with...weird stuff..." Emn buried her face in Atalant's neck and sighed again when Atalant ran fingers through her hair. "I'm just saying that it's always more complicated than we think. Especially with Risalians around."

Yorden patted her shoulder before sitting back down. "There will be one Risalian against the five of us. Three of you can manipulate cellulose *with your minds*. I think the odds are, for once, in our favor."

* * *

Emn sat in the middle of the long, plush bench in the *Lucidity*'s lounge, wedged tightly between Atalant and

Nicholas. Salice sat on the other side of Nicholas; her face creased into a scowl. Yorden waited outside the ship, in the hangar bay, for the arrival of Captain Ran's progenitor, Wan, whom Emn *really* just wanted to shoot in the face. It was just an exam. That's what everyone kept telling her. That's what she kept telling herself. Just an exam to make sure she was all right. A final effort to salvage their first vacation.

Yet, no one spoke. Memories from Salice bled together with Emn's own, sinking her mood further. Nicholas had stopped cracking jokes over an hour ago, and even Atalant's hand on her thigh failed to distract.

Ran.

Emn still had a billion emotions tied to the Risalian captain, even if she had shot hir dead herself and then burned everyone on hir ship. Every footfall on the braided carpet of the *Lucidity* felt like her mother's heartbeat. Every sniffle, every throat clearing, was an echo from Ran's cutter. She could spend a lifetime running from those memories, or a lifetime drowning in them. *Confronting* them had never been on the list.

The door to the lounge slid open. Yorden entered first, turning ever so slightly to the side to pass through. Emn caught a flash of blue before she looked at the floor—lost herself in the yellow and orange weave of the carpet that surrounded her toes. Her heart hammered in her chest. Atalant's fingers dug into her skin, although what an eld of Ardulum had to fear from a Risalian scientist, Emn couldn't begin to guess.

She heard Yorden pull two chairs forward, and then there were blue feet in her range of vision, the toes ending in curved, black claws. Emn drew her eyes up, her brow wrinkling as she did so. Red cotton pants with a white drawstring. A bare chest with pale-blue skin showed a patchwork of iridescent purple scales. The Risalian's cheeks were sunken below hir cheekbones, hir lips were thin and drawn into a tight line, and hir hair was a shocking white.

Yorden inclined his head at Wan. "As we discussed, this is Wan, the progenitor of Ran and the former head of Cell-Tal."

Because of course Ran's family was alive. Of course, they were also entrenched in Cell-Tal. Of course, Yorden couldn't have found a Risalian—*any* Risalian—unaffiliated with the being who had killed her mother and had controlled every aspect of her existence.

"Emn," Wan greeted when her eyes finally met the Risalian's. Xe inclined hir head, leaned forward slowly—so slowly that it seemed comical—and placed a leather bag onto hir lap. "Yorden has already inspected the contents. Would you like to as well?"

Emn flashed her eyes to Yorden.

"They're legit, as far as I can tell. Genome sequencer. Handheld X-ray thing. Couple of computers with lasers. All with a ton of cellulose. You could melt them in a heartbeat."

"Tempting." Emn glared at Wan. "Why are you in red?" she demanded. "Why are *you* here?"

A soft, sad, little smile ghosted across Wan's face. Emn snorted.

"I'm a scientist, Emn. *Just* a scientist. You've only...rather, all you were ever allowed to see was the military side. The Risalians aren't just the Markin and the captains. We're not even Cell-Tal. Most of us are just...beings. Beings trying to live and make a contribution." With hir eyes steadily on Emn's, Wan lifted the flap of the bag and took out a flat piece of biofilm the thickness and width of Emn's pinkie finger. Xe handed it to Emn, who refused to take it.

Wan's voice softened. "I resigned from Cell-Tal the day Ran died. I'm here because Yorden put in a call to the Markin Council for the Risalian most familiar with your creation. I can best assess whether or not anything is amiss. I have no blessing from Cell-Tal, nor do they know I am here. However, I still have access to all their archives. I *built* most of their tech."

"You built *me*," Emn spat.

Wan nodded. "With Ran, yes. I built you. But thanks to the files Eld Atalant provided, I have the original Ardulan base code, too. If you'll put this biofilm on your forehead, the diagnostics will only take a few minutes. Combined with Keft and Neek genetics, we should be able to figure out how to fine-tune your telepathy to access this new frequency you're hearing."

"Her head isn't a radio," Nicholas interjected, sourly. "You're making this sound too easy."

"It *is* simple. She's a standard mammalian biped, just like you." Xe held up the biofilm as calmly as if they were all having breakfast coffee. There wasn't even a hint of purpling at hir neck slits. "This could sequence your unique genome in an hour. I could cure you of any genetic condition in two. We may not have the *ethics* quite down, but the science is sound."

"But you could just, like, put that on and reprogram her then!" Nicholas stood and glared. "This is a terrible idea."

"Fun thing about that though." Atalant's hand slid from Emn's knee and snaked around her waist. Emn smiled smugly. "The Aggression Talent is so flexible. I get even a sense of danger from Emn, and Wan gets classified as a weapon. Then, *I* get to melt hir."

This time, Wan's neck did flush. "I came here to help."

"Which is probably all that's keeping you alive right now," Yorden countered. He turned to Emn. "This whole thing is ridiculous on a galactic scale. I get it."

Emn had too many conflicting emotions swirling in her gut to respond. Yorden was an amazing captain. An amazing friend. But he hadn't lived her life. He'd lived *a* life, and it had been hard, she knew, but this was... His past was locked away on some backwater planet. He'd successfully avoided it for over half his lifetime. Emn did not have that luxury.

"I don't want to be here," Emn finally managed to mutter.

Yorden pursed his lips and nodded. "Yeah. I get that. But I also get the Risalians, Emn. I know them way better than I ever wanted to, and I know that when they don't wear tunics...they're opting out. Like me. Like us. Xe isn't a *good* person, but xe isn't actively engaged in morally reprehensible behavior, either—not that any of us really have the blank record to judge that. And we need you sorted. Give hir a chance, okay? If xe fucks up, we shoot hir."

Emn's jaw set. "I hate you," she said to Wan.

"I know."

"I wish your entire species was galactic sludge."

"Sometimes, so do I."

"There is no way you can ever atone for what you did."

Wan's neck slits resumed their normal color. "That doesn't mean I shouldn't try."

"Fine." Emn slumped back against Atalant, her eyes narrowed. Wan leaned in, and Emn felt the faintest brush of claw against her forehead before a wet, viscous substance adhered to her skin. She shivered.

"It will only take a moment," Wan whispered unnecessarily.

It had only taken a moment for Ran to shoot her mother, too.

Still, Emn felt...nothing unusual from the device. She waited, Atalant's fingers now wrapped tightly around her upper arm. Nicholas's eyes darted from hers to Wan's and then back again. Another two breaths, and the small device flaked from her forehead into Wan's waiting hand.

You okay? Atalant asked as Wan fed the biofilm strip into a genome reader.

I...I think it just collected some skin cells, honestly, Emn returned. *Definitely no interfacing.*

You're still pretty tense, love.

Emn snorted. *Part of that might be because you're cutting off the circulation in my arm.*

Atalant loosened her grip, sliding her hand down to Emn's elbow and then finally to her hand. Her fingers were sticky—Atalant's fingers were always sticky—but Emn felt the *stuk* thickening back to its normal texture.

Emn looked back at Atalant and smiled. "Better."

"A lot of coding in here," Wan muttered, likely more loudly than xe intended. "I'd forgotten how complex it'd gotten by the time we bred your mother."

Emn's back stiffened.

"Maybe we could bypass the husbandry language?" Yorden said in that dangerous, gruff voice Emn rarely heard him use. Wan missed the tone entirely.

"Science is often callous, especially when translated. I'm not actively trying to offend. I'm just trying to... Here!" The device in Wan's hand chirped, and the Risalian looked up, triumphant. "I'd forgotten. We opened your telepathic bridgeway entirely. All telepathic species in your greater genus have this little...organ, for lack of a better word, right near your brain stem. It has a species-specific casing that works like a filter. It's one of the big ways we can tell a Neek from a Keft, or from an Ardulan, etcetera."

Wan pointed at Atalant. "The casing is naturally sort of thick. Species with empathic mucus use this feature to amplify transmission. Like a coupling agent that reduces static. The more you breed with Ardulans, the more the natural casing degrades. Ardulans have one, of course, but it's all full of holes. But *you*, Emn—" Wan held out the device. Emn wrinkled her nose as she looked at it, but the text scrolling across was so technical that, even though it was in Common, she couldn't parse it. "We managed to completely remove yours. In theory, you could hear any subspecies. Any genetically compatible relative."

"Okay, but how does that help me?" Emn sat forward and slapped the device from Wan's hands. Hir neck slits tinged momentarily purple, but xe didn't retrieve the scanner. "I don't want to be a beacon. I don't *want* to hear every distress call from every subspecies. I *want* to be normal."

Wan's tongue flicked over hir lower lip. Xe rubbed at hir neck with one long claw, the sound something akin to a dish from Earth that Yorden liked called squeaky cheese.

Emn hated squeaky cheese.

"I can help refine your telepathy, but I can't fix it because there is nothing broken. This is what you were made to be."

Emn had tried so hard in the past year to find a place for herself on Ardulum. A place for herself with Atalant. Working with Corccinth's flares and Arik and talking to Ardulum had caused that open wound of otherness to scab over, but now she was bleeding again. And this time, sweet words and tearing Atalant out of her clothes wouldn't be enough to stop the flow.

Emn shot to her feet, pushing away from Atalant's hands. "I need some space."

"Emn!" Atalant called, but Emn stalked to the other end of the lounge and through the door that would take her to the main hatch and out into the spaceport. She looked back at the concerned eyes of the crew and narrowed her connection with Atalant to a whisper.

"I don't need platitudes from a Risalian!" she yelled back. "You figure out how to give me a filter, or at the very least a tracking option so I can *find* anyone who calls me, or get the fuck out of my life!"

Emn threw open the main hatch as loudly as she was able and jumped the four steps to the floor of the docking bay. Her bare feet hit with a painful smack, but she didn't care. *Fuck* Risalians and their uselessness. Fuck them for making her feel like an experiment. She could be surrounded by a billion subspecies, and she'd still be the one bred in a lab.

Atalant tugged at her mind.

I'm fine, she sent. *I just need, like, an hour to process. I'm coming back, just...give me a little air.*

Atalant reluctantly backed away.

She slammed her bare feet onto the floor, letting the sharp tingles of metal on flesh ground her. This was

Yorden's private hangar, but it was easily big enough to fit five or six more tramp ships. He'd mostly used it for "excess" haul storage over the years, so towers of crates and boxes littered the floor. It was the perfect place to punch things, kick things, and generally vent her frustrations without anyone trying to calm her down.

"I'm so tired of being like this!" Emn kicked a small cardboard box. A tinkling sound came from inside as it skittered across the floor.

"Is this a bad time?"

Emn jumped at the voice, landing against a marble statue of some Terran without clothes in an awkward pose. She turned toward the voice, rubbing her hip. A mass of orange curls peeked out from a pile of stacked paper books tall enough to kill a biped if it collapsed. August waved tentatively and offered a sheepish grin.

"I'm not creepy, I swear. I was coming to find you and saw you storm from the ship. I wasn't sure how to approach, what with all the kicking."

Emn sighed and rubbed her temples. "Why are you looking for me? I know we were pretty clear at the bar."

August's mouth opened and then snapped shut. Their brows furrowed. "This isn't a pickup. I wanted to ask you this at the bar, but your girlfriend stunned me a bit. But I guess she would, right? She's Eld Atalant?"

Now, it was Emn's turn to gape. Ardulan culture—and Neek culture, for that matter—barely registered as a blip in the Charted Systems. Atalant was still easily recognizable as Exile, but few outside the Neek homeworld would know of her recent...promotion.

"Who *are* you?" Emn asked.

August's head bobbed left to right, taking in the otherwise deserted hangar, and then held out their hand. "An explorer," they said in a whisper. "An orphan of a planet that died the moment Ardulum appeared in the sky."

Emn stared at the Terran's hands. They wore thin leather gloves, which Emn hadn't noticed before, but bulging underneath...

August nodded and pulled the gloves off their wrists. The skin matched the gloves, but at the end, where nails should have been, bloomed multicolored feathers.

"Oh," Emn breathed, the frustrations from minutes before slipping from her muscles. "You're..."

"A genetic cousin," August finished. "And I've come a really long way to find Ardulum—and you."

Emn stared at the feathers as the dream she shared with August pieced back together in her mind. She studied the bleed of the colors, the angle of the downy barbs, the way the structure melted into mammalian flesh right where a fingernail might end. It was so much easier to contemplate the genetics of avian and mammalian crossing than to figure out what to say to someone you only knew through screams and feathers and the memory of a crumbling planet.

"I'm sorry," August said, finally filling the silence. "I didn't think... I didn't think this would be that big of a surprise. I've been traveling the Charted Systems for a number of months. I've been to Neek and heard the stories. I mean, I even watched a holo of Eld Atalant flying an old settee with the Heaven Guard pilots during the big fires. I was led to understand there was a sort of...reconciliation afoot. Or, at the very least, that Ardulum wasn't hiding from its children anymore."

Emn slowly moved her gaze up, following the thin, silver flower stenciled on the sleeve of August's shirt. The collar of the shirt was white, the skin touching the collar a pale pink. From there, Emn followed the heavy dusting of brown and orange freckles to August's tilted head and arched eyebrows.

A refugee from an exploded planet that likely had gone the way of Keft. Atalant would explode half the *Lucidity* when she found out.

"We, uh," Emn stumbled for words. "We're on vacation."

August blinked. "That's why you're destroying containers in a cluttered ship berth?"

Emn felt her face flush. "I've been picking up your nightmares, I think. We weren't sure what was going on, and it meant we had to import someone I hate to figure out what was wrong with me." She tried to force a smile, but it likely came out more as a grimace. "It would have been nice to have gotten an explanation from you at the bar."

This time, August flushed, the red creeping from their— no, if August was from a seeded planet, then it would be zir—zir neck to forehead. "I didn't realize who you were until Eld Atalant came over and then... Ardulum is a legend to my people. Not a religion, like on Neek, but still. Meeting an eld of Ardulum, especially one I'd just heard spoken about like she was a literal god, overwhelmed me. I'd also just hit on her girlfriend and really didn't want to be impaled by a piece of andal."

The corner of August's mouth quirked up, and Emn nodded in amused agreement. "Yeah, that was a good call." She clasped her hands behind her back, her anger slipping away. "Is there something you need from us? Did you just want to meet us? Your planet—" She paused, unsure how best to word the question. "Your planet is beyond help at this point, correct? Are there people who need aid?" Emn thought of the rounded shadow in the dream. "Ardulum only came the once? Or, did it actually come as your planet burned? Because that's..." She was going to say, "cold even for Ardulum," but the truth was, that was probably no worse than half a dozen other things the planet had done.

"Oh, no." August sat on a cardboard box marked *DEFINITELY NOT FRAGILE IN ANY WAY*. "That was my brain being weird, I think. As to your other question, I've got one of our scouting ships out on research. I'm an explorer, as I mentioned. We have a branch of scientists that works sort of like the Heaven Guard. We know we are a blend of two different species. It's been a mission of ours for almost a century to find that second species, but we are from a long ways away. Tesseracts are great, but they still take time over incredible distances and, of course, Ardulum travels."

"You're the first one to make it to the Charted Systems?" Emn asked. She'd never really thought of the Systems as being backwater, but then again, she didn't give a lot of thought to the layout of the universe, either.

"Yes. We'd made it to the Alliance, of course—it's much larger and closer to us—but that was before Ardulum came there, so we missed it. And the Charted Systems are particularly difficult to navigate since you use wormholes instead of drives of any kind, so your allied systems are not in any particular arrangement. Earth is actually the closest, which is where I started and, consequently"—they waved their feathered hand—"the reason for the gloves. Terrans are surprisingly xenophobic. Besides, it became clear that there wasn't a lot of bipedal diversity in the Systems."

"And then you found Neek," Emn concluded, trying to imagine both the arrival on Earth and then the stumbling onto the equally religiously fervent Neek.

"It's not a lot of fun to stick out around here."

"Heh." Emn rubbed her temples. "I know. I suppose if you know about Atalant, then I'm guessing you know about my history?"

August sat back and regarded Emn curiously. "You're Ardulan. Was there something else?"

Exasperated, Emn held up her arms so that August could clearly see the intersecting geometric veins that melded just underneath her skin.

August frowned and then lifted up zir shirt. Emn froze. Zir freckles were much more ordered on the skin of zir belly, spinning into patterns and forms Emn knew all too well. Triangles. Hexagons. Geometric patterns spanned down into actual Talent markings on zir side and scattered into flare nonsense everywhere else.

Coloring aside, zie looked just like Emn.

Emn brought her arms down and sat down on the box next to August. She ran a hand through her short, auburn hair, her mind spiraling like disordered cellulose.

"Do all your people have that?" she finally managed. "Those markings?"

"Not in the same place," August responded matter-of-factly. "Some have more, some less. Some are completely covered, like you. Some just have a few freckles on their face. Historically, it wasn't very prevalent at all, but we had to do some genetic tinkering to survive on the planet we colonized when Rithorununun failed, and these cropped up as a result. More is considered fashionable." Zir voice softened. "They're a mark of beauty. It's why I first sought you out in the bar. Even if they'd just been tattoos, they'd still be pretty."

"You... Beauty? Genetic tinkering? You did this to yourselves? To survive?" She had so, so many questions, but...Risalian biotechnology. Ran's work. They hadn't introduced *anything*. They hadn't *made* anything. They'd turned things on and turned things off and combined phenotypes until Emn had been unrecognizable, but she *was still a person.*

August took her hand and traced a thumb over the dark lines of Emn's palm. Emn shivered—not from arousal, but surprise. August was... Zie wasn't reverent, exactly. Zie was...comfortable? Validated? No. None of those words were right.

"I'm sorry, Emn," August said in a near whisper, zir thumb pressing ever so slightly against Emn's skin. Emn felt August's mind brush hers—feathery, polite—a request for entrance. Emn slid her mind back like one would move away from a swinging door and let August step inside.

I'm sorry I broadcasted and ruined your vacation. At puberty, we start taking a certain plant extract that limits our dream telepathy range. I'd stopped taking it because there weren't any of my people this far out. I know my nightmares... I've been seeing someone for them, for the post-traumatic stress, but it never occurred to me that someone else could hear them. Zie paused. *Probably because I didn't think there would be other subspecies. Besides Neek, anyway. I guess we're all pretty myopic in that way.*

Why do you dream about your planet exploding? Emn asked.

Sadness laced with fear danced across their link. *We'd left the planet a century ago because it failed. The andal failed, then the ecosystem failed, and then the planet failed. It failed to be breathable, habitable—everything—but it was still there. I'm not just an explorer—I'm an archeologist. I was there doing a solo dig that day because my assistant was sick. We never...we never thought the planet might be unstable. I barely got off in time.*

In the memories and emotions that chased August's words, Emn caught the undercurrent of context. August shouldn't have been there. Being on the planet wasn't allowed, but zie had ignored the law and gone anyway, and it had almost killed zir.

"But I found something finally, didn't I?" August said. Zir voice felt too loud in the quiet bay, even buffered as they were by so many old packages covered in Yorden's sprawling handwriting.

"Yes, you did." Emn stood, keeping hold of August's hand, and tugged zir in the direction of the *Lucidity*. She'd never been great at keeping her emotions from leaking over to Atalant, and so, unsurprisingly, she felt a hesitant, questioning presence in the back of her mind. Emn laughed to herself because she felt like a settee pilot on her first mission, like an Ardulan flare peeling off their makeup and walking through the capital. Most importantly, she felt *kinship*, because she might be unique as a Risalian Ardulan flare whatever, but it wasn't anything the Risalians had done. It was what they'd *undone,* and she, like August, was exactly who she was meant to be.

"Emn?" August asked.

"Would you like to come meet them?"

Confusion crossed August's face. "Meet them? Meet whom?"

Emn grinned widely enough to feel it in her ears. "Would you like to come meet my family?"

* * *

Silence could be a spiny thing, Emn decided. Silence could prickle and jab and poke you in places you never thought about, especially when the silence was shared between everyone you loved.

But silence made sense, too, because really, what was anyone going to say?

Atalant sat next to her on the long plush bench in the game room of the *Lucidity*, Nicholas to her left. Salice stood near the far wall, and Yorden barred the door, his hand alternating between tapping the wall and smoothing his beard.

August stood before them all, shifting zir weight and failing to not look nervous. Even the Risalian asshole was still around, but in this moment, Emn didn't mind. She felt too good, too light, to let one Risalian ruin things.

There'd been a lot of words already—words on the boarding ramp, words in the hallway, words while Atalant paced across the game room while Emn tried to calm her down. Because yes, August's existence brought a lot of questions—but it'd brought a lot of much-needed answers, too.

That feeling was better than sex with Atalant. Well, almost.

But now was the time for more technical discussions. The planet Rithorununun had been seeded over four centuries ago according to the Ardulan calendar Atalant had dug up. It was long enough ago that there were no star charts available and the name of the solar system it inhabited didn't match any database they could access.

Wan's genetic reader had proved similarly useless. August's genetic code had too much drift for the little portable device. Several attempts to use it had almost drained the battery, leaving Wan cranky but intrigued.

Nicholas was the only one of them who was asking the questions Emn thought were important, although even he seemed shell-shocked. Maybe that was maturity, Emn mused, or maybe it was a reaction to absurdity, especially since August had pretended to be human. Still, there could be no doubt now about zir genetics. Delicate feathers no longer than Emn's thumbnail sprouted from every one of August's ten fingers. The quill of each feather was blue, the downy barbs purple, and the main barbs a forest green.

Nicholas stumbled over his next question. He'd tried to ask it several times already, muttering a "never mind" halfway through each attempt. Emn understood. She'd seen the planet explode firsthand. Talking about its former inhabitants seemed callous.

"There, um, how many?" Nicholas finally managed. "How many got off Rithorununun? Or, was it completely evacuated when it exploded?"

August scratched zir ear with the tip of a feather. "Most of the population was off. There were just a few science stations left, so maybe a few hundred? The government still gave out a few permits back then, but not to everyone. I don't know. We've had colonies on other worlds for over a century, just none in the Charted Systems or the Alliance. I'm the first to make it out this far. Ardulum—"

Atalant cut zir off. "We're well aware of what Ardulum is capable of, and what it's done."

With that, the crew again fell to silence.

Zie isn't the enemy, Atalant, Emn gently reminded her. *And we don't know why Ritho-whatever exploded.*

Bet we know why the Rithani had colonies off-world though, Atalant shot back, her tone biting. *We've seen Keft. We didn't know how that ecological chain of events ends until now.*

Emn tried to steel her emotions. Atalant was jumping to—the admittedly correct—conclusions. Despite the progress Atalant had made with her Talents, Emn felt the other woman's temper edging dangerously near to exploding something. This wasn't a time for explosions and tension and guilt over things Atalant had no control over. Damn it, she'd get this crew on the right track even if she had to beat them all with andal to do it.

You are not responsible for the mistakes of Ardulum, Emn reminded her. *And Ritho-whatever and Keft and all the other seeded planets are not Neek.*

"But they're all my responsibility." Atalant stood and loomed over August. Emn saw the crease in her brow and the purse of her lips and closed her eyes in exasperation. Reparations-Atalant was much harder to calm down than why-is-there-no-bacon-I'm-not-eating-andal-again Atalant. "How many more refugees are we going to stumble across? How many thousands of worlds has Ardulum destroyed? We *have* to fix things."

August crossed zir arms and snorted. "We're not broken, Eld Atalant. I didn't come here looking for help, just facts."

Atalant bristled at the title. She always did, but it seemed like it was a particularly sharp barb today. "*You have no planet.*"

August smoothed a wrinkle on zir pants and pursed zir mouth. Emn could hear zir breath catch, saw the color drain from zir face. "We don't need help. We could have used it a century ago, but that's long past. I just want to talk to you. Both of you. See Ardulum, if that's possible. I... Our planet is beyond help."

Out of the corner of her eye, Emn saw Atalant grow still, mind going blank.

"You've never wanted to see if your myths were true?" August prodded, stroking one of zir feather nails. "Never wanted to see if you could find your myths in a vast universe of possibilities?"

Emn saw Atalant's *stuk* start to drip and smothered a smile.

"You don't make any sense." Atalant slumped back onto the bench. Emn refrained from pointing out that, a year ago, she and Atalant had made their own pilgrimage to

Ardulum. Atalant knew that well enough. Pushing down emotions had always been her initial instinct.

August laughed. "From one colonized subspecies to another, neither do you. Do you always leak fluids?"

Atalant sat up sharply. "You don't secrete empathic mucus?"

"We might have at one point, but I'm sure that would have been one of the first genes we'd have switched off."

Emn cut off Atalant's retort. "You'd be surprised how many uses it has," she quipped, making sure her eye contact with Atalant was long enough to convey the layers of meaning. Atalant's face flushed.

"Mucus or not, August is certainly a subspecies," Wan said as xe finally looked up from hir genetic coder, a look on hir face that Emn couldn't quite place. "Though, I assume that is not your given name."

Emn frowned. "No?"

August looked sheepish. "Aruninuntn is my given name, and I've got six family names. August will work fine unless Ardulans are used to polysyllabic names?" Zie turned to Atalant. "Are there a lot of subspecies on Ardulum? I can't even imagine what it looks like. What a thrill, to encounter a fairy tale!"

Atalant's shoulder bumped into Emn's, hard enough that Emn could tell Atalant was slumping. She understood the tension, but still, the similarities of their situations were very nearly comical. Under a different set of circumstances, Emn wondered if Ardulum wouldn't have ended up with Eld Aruninuntn—if the andal had had a specific subspecies in mind or if any wandering, seeking, voyaging one would have worked to shake up Ardulan politics.

August wasn't unattractive. Emn thought about that possibility, briefly. A different path to the same ending.

I am open to an eventual gatoi partner in this relationship if that's what you want, but not that gatoi, Atalant sent firmly.

Emn bit her lower lip and stifled a giggle. This was an opening that was too good to miss because, while there were many types of relationships on Neek and Ardulum, it wasn't uncommon to add a gatoi to a same-gender relationship if procreation was on the table.

I didn't realize you wanted children.

Atalant's eyes widened so much that Emn briefly worried that they might pop out from Atalant's head. Atalant snatched her hand from Emn's, her *stuk* already as thin as water, and shook her head violently.

No. No no no no no. That is not how this story ends.

Atalant backed herself up against a wall, her eyes bouncing from accusing to terrified. This was a lot for her. It was a lot for all of them, but the severity was unfounded. August wanted genealogy, nothing more. Zie wanted history and understanding, and maybe to see a few million more beings that looked like zir. Emn got it. Atalant needed that, too.

"Atalant." Ignoring everyone else staring at Atalant like she had grown a second head, Emn grabbed Atalant's hand and guided her back to the bench. She put her hands on Atalant's shoulders, pushed her down, and then dropped, firmly, onto Atalant's lap.

Emn?

Emn wrapped her legs around Atalant's waist, ignoring the mental surprise and protest. Who cared that everyone was watching? She put her hands on Atalant's cheeks and kissed her.

Atalant's mind fell silent. Nicholas coughed and Yorden chuckled, but Emn only wove them closer together— tongues, hands, minds.

Emn? Atalant asked again as Emn felt the tension start to drain from Atalant's shoulders.

You can spend the rest of your don *mopping up Ardulum's mistakes or making new ones of your own. There will always be people that need you and crises that have to be averted. This isn't one of them, but even if it was, you know what?* Emn pulled back just enough so that she could kiss Atalant's chin. Then, she touched the tip of her nose to Atalant's and delighted in the smile that broke across Atalant's face.

What? Atalant returned. Her mental voice sounded so hopeful, so earnest, that Emn's heart leaped with a joy that a year ago she'd have thought impossible.

How we got here, to this place, together. I don't think it was the Risalians' doing, or the Neek's. I don't think this story is about Ardulum, even, or the andal or god. Gods. Whatever.

Atalant's eyebrow rose. "The facts and events would suggest—"

"Think about everything that has happened. Think about where we are. This has all been about us finding each other, Atalant. We are how the story ends. Right here. Because it's a love story."

"Hear! Hear!" Yorden called as he moved forward and offered an arm to Salice. She took it, and Nicholas stood and joined them, a big cheesy grin spread across his face.

"Love means different things to different people, and it's not always about romance, but yeah—I think she's right, Atalant." Nicholas did his best to flop back down on the bench and then scooted right into Atalant and Emn. Wan coughed loudly and made a hasty retreat from the ship.

Emn wrapped her right arm around Nicholas and pulled him into the embrace. Atalant grunted good-naturedly even as Salice pushed into their other side and Yorden's arms encompassed them all.

"This is so cheesy," Atalant murmured.

"And mildly unexpected," August added.

Yorden thumped Atalant on the top of her head. "Shut up, you love it. You love it as much as I love it. We're a goddamned family, Atalant. With you here, we don't even need to go to synagogue. Most realistic utopia I've ever been sold—even if you do curse an awful lot."

Atalant shot him an incredulous look. "I didn't even *know* Common curse words before I met you."

Yorden gave his best innocent face. "I'm a paragon of virtue, lady. I have no idea what you are talking about."

"Fuck you, Yorden."

Yorden turned to smirk at Salice, who gave him a scrunched-nose smile in return. He winked at Emn before looking back at Atalant. "We're always going to have all this shit to do and people who need us and fucking worlds that rely on us. That's just the nature of things. It sucks, but it only takes as much as you give it."

Emn leaned in and whispered into Atalant's ear, "You're mine, Atalant." Atalant blushed. Her *stuk* started to gel on Emn's arms. "You're mine, and this is our ending. Right here. Everything else is just—"

"Appendices," Nicholas cut in. He smirked when Emn glared at him. "Oh, come on. I had to. 'Cause this isn't the *end* end. Just, you know, the end of one story. And Atalant got the girl—or Emn did, whatever—and Salice got the man, and I got a bunch of amazing friends. What more could anyone want?"

Atalant laughed—a cheerful, throaty laugh—and Emn felt her whole face break into a smile. Their eyes met, and in them, Emn saw hundreds of futures, each difficult but refracting hope.

"Okay," Atalant said, so low that Emn wasn't certain anyone else heard it. "I'm calm. I'm relaxing. It's vacation again."

"About damn time!" Yorden broke his hold on them, nudged Nicholas to the side with a hairy foot, and looked expectantly at Emn while his eyes twinkled mischief. She grinned and slid off Atalant. The moment her bottom hit the bench, Yorden had Atalant by the arm and was dragging her upright and toward the exit.

"Yorden! What?"

"Vacation!" Yorden barked. He opened the hatch and towed a confused Atalant behind him down the ramp.

Nicholas shot Emn a questioning look. She shrugged and queried Salice, but the answer she received was smug and nonsensical. Unsure of what else to do, she got up and followed them, Nicholas, Salice, and August trailing behind.

"Come if you want, August!" Yorden yelled back as they exited the private berth into throngs of beings in the arterial hallway. "We're always up for a new crewmate, but this is all just a bit too serious, and we've got a show to catch."

"A show?" Emn called up, trying not to get slimed by an Oorin family.

"Cabaret!" Yorden said enthusiastically.

"Minoran again?" Nicholas asked, wrinkling his nose.

Yorden stopped dead in the middle of the walkway, eliciting a number of curses from irate sentients. His mouth quirked into a lopsided grin, his untamed beard pointed in two different directions, and his eyes glittered impishly. "Better."

"Human?" August asked cautiously as zie edged into the crowd.

"Better." He dropped Atalant's arm, wiped his hand on his pants, and then brought his hands together to make an O shape. "Mmnnuggl. Mmnnuggl cabaret. There are skirts. You'll love it."

This time, he offered Atalant a hand, which she took, a wide smile on her face. Emn came up and took her other hand, and then Nicholas took Emn's. And it was stupid, and cliché, and as sappy as Yorden on his fifth whiskey shot—and Emn *loved it*.

"Come on, everyone," Yorden said, pulling the chain of them toward the station transport. "It's time to have some fun."

BA
TO
WA

Like many of the stories in TALES, this is meant as a fluffy, feel-good story. Is it canon? It can be. Mostly it's a glimpse of Atalant and Emn away from ruling, away from Ardulum, getting to connect with one of my favorite pastimes.

Quality Time

"I don't understand," Emn said. "Where are we again?"

Atalant shrugged and spun in a slow circle. Flashing lights. Loud music. Some type of mechanical animatronic...animals? In front of her, on the counter was a plastic pitcher of beer—that at least was familiar—a basket of strong-smelling stick bread, and a handful of gold-colored coins that Atalant was *very* certain were not a form of galactic standard currency. It looked, very nearly, like one of the pleasure casinos of the Charted Systems, but here the dancers were robots and the gambling items were shorter—designed for Oori perhaps? Small Minorans?

"I think...I think it's a bar?" She'd hoped to sound more certain.

"Humans aren't this short though," Emn said, kneeling so she could better grab a plastic joystick very similar to the control system of the old *Pledge*. "I wish it wasn't so loud." She turned back to stare at the clacking plastic animals, whose mouths moved out of sync with the music. "When Nicholas suggested a night out of 'classic Americana,' I thought...I mean I don't know what I thought but I didn't think it'd be an empty bar."

Atalant gathered the pitcher, the bread, and the coins onto a round tray and walked to a table. This, at least, looked familiar. Emn followed, her eyes wide, the flashing red and yellow lights giving her skin a candied glow. "Yorden said they booked the place for the night," Atalant said, "so we could get the full experience without the crowd. But Yorden *likes* crowds, so I don't know."

"Also why aren't they here?" Emn slid into the booth, a *whoosh* of depressed air following. "It's hard underneath. This isn't comfortable."

"Maybe it's so you don't stay too long? Or game more?"

"Maybe." Emn smoothed the blue denim pants across her thighs, and Atalant caught her nose wrinkle at the stiffness. Clothes, too, had been critical, according to Nicholas. *Jeans* were critical. But Emn's were too loose for Atalant's liking and her own felt too tight, and the gaudy white t-shirts they both wore that said "SIX FLAGS GREAT AMERICA" still smelled like a forgotten closet on the *Pledge*.

"They said they'd join us later, after the game. I don't know what game. There are games *here,* so maybe a more competitive game. With a ball." Atalant smiled sheepishly. "They like the one with the oblong ball, the brown one. Which," she sighed, "we have sports on Neek but balls there are actually ball shaped. Terrans have issues. I don't like balls anyway. Piloting is my skill, not tossing pieces of titha hide around."

"We did agree to come here." Emn took a bite of breadstick, wrinkled her nose, then delicately spat into her paper napkin. "No. I did not agree to whatever that is."

Atalant sniffed, decided to take Emn's word for it, and sipped the flat beer instead. "So. Vacation. Earth. What uh, what do you want to do tomorrow?"

Emn, still tracing the multiple strings of flashing lights, rubbed her temples. "Not this?"

"Do you want to just go?"

Emn's eyes locked to Atalant's and a firm internal voice said, *Yes. Now.*

Thank andal for girlfriends that liked a night in as much as she did. Atalant slid from the booth and was almost to her feet when a Mmnnuggl floated over to them, ear tips so deeply red that Atalant had a hard time believing the youth was out of puberty. Another round, brown tray balanced on his head, and on the tray were two clear plastic cups.

The sphere set the tray down onto the table in an elaborate dip and shimmy movement.

"Are you having fun?" the Mmnnuggl teenager asked.

"We uh, are ready to go now. Thank you though."

The sphere dipped, red ears phasing to purple. "Oh. I messed something up, didn't I?"

"No!" Emn shot to her feet, hands waving. "You've been great. You got us the gold coins and the...bread. And new cups! Wow they're...clean. But we have another appointment."

"Could you stay maybe just a little longer?" The Mmnnuggl sat on the floor and rotated to "look" up at them. "My parents like me to work at least five hours every weekend. It's good experience for college. I'm in my last year of high school and I know books are expensive. I just want to not have a ton of student loans, you know? And I get paid by the hour here."

Atalant was going to have to sit with that for a moment before she could formulate a coherent thought.

"Oh!" The sphere puffed a meter upwards in...joy? "I'm adopted. That's what you were wondering, wasn't it? You know like, since the Charted Systems and the Alliance started working together more and the Alliance adopted the Youth Journey program, a lot of other things have gone intergalactic. Human parents are cool. You're human, aren't you?"

"No, but our friends are," said Emn, admitting defeat and sitting back down in the booth.

Atalant took the new cups and poured the beer in, half filling, because there was no need to torture themselves. Emn's hand hovered over her bit-off breadstick. The sphere all but bounced off the floor. "Yay! Thank you so much! I'm Jeff and you just holler if you need anything, okay?"

"Thank you. Jeff." Atalant smiled, showing more of her teeth than she'd planned but forced smiles never looked pretty. Jeff, ears now back to full red, turned a tight 360 and floated back around to the front of the store.

They were left with each other, the smell of borderline palatable food, and the giant animatronic animals on stage.

"Maybe it's a horror house?" Emn asked in a whisper. "Nicholas went to an escape room yesterday, I'm assuming because he's never been actually locked in a tight space he couldn't get out of. Maybe this is like...that?"

"Maybe? Either way, I guess we are here for a while. I think we are supposed to be having fun, regardless. Try the breadstick again?"

Emn's eyebrow raised, but while her tone came out harsh, Atalant caught the lilt in her mind. "I can't digest grains, Atalant." She picked up one of the coins and brought it up to her left eye. "Is this one of the ones we eat? Like that candle holiday Yorden celebrates? The one with the spinning top?"

Atalant took another one of the coins and sniffed it. Metallic. Definitely not edible. A token then, which made sense, since one of Yorden's favorite Martian restaurants had a pool table that took silver tokens. "For the games, I think, but I don't see any slot machines. Maybe flying games? Don't know about those though. Unless they're, oh! Maybe they're target games!" She pointed to a row of long, tilted runs with circular holes at the apex and a series of wooden balls in a slot near the right side. "Bar with games. I get it now! And the animals are...labor laws? Maybe humans aren't allowed to perform? We can ask later." She took a long, disgusting drink of the beer, poured the remainder from her glass back into the pitcher because there was no *way* she was drinking more of that, and offered Emn a hand. "Want to play?"

Emn poked a finger into the bread and pinched her mouth to the side when her finger left a soft indent. "Yes?"

"Wonderful." Atalant scooped the tokens into her pocket and stood. She offered Emn a hand, which the younger woman took with a bright smile—damn, there was never going to be a time when Emn couldn't melt her with that smile—and together they walked to the target game. The word SKEE-BALL lit across the wall, blinking in neon yellow. Atalant put a token into the slot and a whole mess of lights sprang to life on the machine. Horrible, ear-grating music started, and several additional wooden balls dropped into the slot on the right side.

"This is a ball game," Emn commented wryly. "Yorden and Nicholas could have come."

"No, it's a *target* game. I can fly us through asteroid fields in a piece of titha shit ship so," Atalant picked up one of the balls, passed it between her hands which thoroughly covered it in *stuk*, and continued. "How hard can this be?" She brought her arm back and threw the ball, overhand, at the center of the raised plastic bullseye.

She hit the rim of the "20" ring. Hard. It shot back out at Atalant and Emn, and they both ducked, but not fast enough. The ball *should* have hit Emn directly in the shoulder, but with Atalant's panic and poorly contained Talent, it puffed to dust on contact, the remnants scattering to the floor.

I don't think that's how you play the game, Emn sent.

Atalant's arm was still protectively around her shoulders, so Emn shrugged out of the embrace. *Want to try again, or shall we try a steadier hand and cooler head?*

Atalant brushed cellulose from Emn's shoulder. "I'm a work in progress."

Emn picked up another ball and frowned. "You have Talent training every week with Corccinth. It's been two years, Atalant. You shouldn't still be randomly exploding things."

Well fuck, now she felt really sheepish. "I am just, *supremely bad* at using my Talents. Any Talents. That's why I have you, remember? You're a natural. I'm a Neek hack in a gold robe."

"If you're cracking jokes, you're relaxing. That's a start." Emn handed the ball to Atalant. "However. I don't think this game is a good use of your natural talents." A smirk crept to the corners of Emn's mouth. "No one else is here and Jeff is hiding in the kitchen or something. He wants us to waste time and I don't want you to destroy every piece of wood in here." She inclined her head. "Put that ball in the 50 circle and we can try something else."

Atalant's *stuk* thickened. She might not have picked up Talent skills, but she was definitely much better now at flirting. "Could you do the activity in fewer clothes?"

Emn glanced at the Skee-Ball bed, then sat with a shrug of her shoulders. "Yes. Especially on a flat surface."

"Jeff!"

A red human ear peered around the corner. "Yes?"

"Could you leave us completely alone for the next hour? Maybe two? You know what, we will just come into the kitchen to get you. Alright?"

A cheerful "Sure!" echoed as an exuberant Jeff bounced away.

Atalant counted to thirty for good measure, before winking at Emn.

"You still haven't gotten the ball in the right repository."

Atalant's hands went to her hips. "You have a lot of demands all of a sudden."

Emn's smile turned syrup-sweet.

"Fine." Atalant regarded the wood ball, remembering the last one coming right at Emn's head, and let her consciousness slip into the part of her brain that dealt with Talents. The ball had tried to hurt Emn. Therefore, the ball had to be a weapon.

"Atalant?" Emn sat on the bed of the adjoining Skee-Ball run. "Nicholas has a bad habit of interrupting us. I appreciate when you take your time on certain activities, but this is not one of them. I'm not that serious about the game. Just take your shirt off."

"You also like it when I'm thorough. Give me just a moment." Chains of crystalline cellulose wound round and round, coated in hemicellulose, structured with lignin. Shaped and ordered but a weapon, too. Atalant tugged a few, reordering and weakening, with no plan or purpose other than sheer destruction. She continued the disordered mayhem to the count of ten, then grabbed the ball she'd been working on from the track and launched it, once again, at the target.

This time when the wood hit it exploded upon impact. A snow of wood dust flitted down, bits falling into each of the circular deposits.

"I win," Atalant said, smugly, as she sat next to Emn and ran a hand under Emn's shirt and around her waist.

Emn kissed Atalant, her tongue flicking over Atalant's lips. *Did you?* As Emn's tongue pushed into her mouth, as Emn's hands pushed Atalant's shirt up, up, over her head, Atalant—in that weird part of her brain that she'd come to realize was distinctly Ardulan—*felt* Emn move the rest of the balls from their slot, roll them up the sloped platform, and deposit them, one at a time, in the 50.

I won you, Emn said. *Now take off the rest of your clothes.*

WHAM WHAM WHAM. The storefront was large bay windows. It was dark outside, but with the interior lighting, that did mean they were distinctly visible to the parking lot.

WHAM WHAM WHAM. A Nicholas-shaped Terran silhouetted, nose pressed against the glass. "This is a children's arcade!" Nicholas glared and stabbed his finger at the window, pointing to the game they were currently sitting on. "And that's not how you play."

A beard materialized next to Nicholas' head, a funnel of hot air frosting the window. "We did get you two a private room at the hotel," Yorden said, his voice strangled in an attempt to not laugh. "I told you, Nick. Women want massages. And if they're into other women, they want massages from *those* women."

"Everyone loves Skee-Ball though!"

Yorden cleared the fog from his breath and stuck an eye right up against the window. "The cords for the miniblinds are in the corners. Maybe you pull those before you continue, huh? We rented the place for the weekend and Jeff in there is legal by Charted Systems standards but maybe you could keep it down. And PG-13."

Atalant stomped to the windows and released the blinds one by one, not bothering to stop their descent and allowing them to clack down onto the tile floor.

"We will see you back at the hotel then," came a farther away version of Nicholas' voice. "Yorden, seriously. You're the one who wanted to check up on them."

"I think that one was pure spite for…something." Atalant nudged back next to Emn. "A…children's arcade. That does explain the game height problems."

"I suppose that means you need to put this back?"

"I guess." The t-shirt found its way back on, Emn's hands repeatedly getting in the way, particularly around the chest area. "We promised Jeff more time though. What do you want to do?"

Emn picked up one of the remaining wood balls and bit into her lower lip. "The purple paper came out when I put the balls in the holes. Right?"

Atalant had completely failed to notice. "Yes? That explains the sign up front about ticket redemption. There must be prizes."

"Hmm." She circled Atalant, lifting the edges of her shirt, tugging at the pockets of her jeans. After two laps she said, "How many tickets for your pants? At the hotel, I mean. I'll cash in there. You'll have to earn mine, too, but I'll make mine cheaper since you only get points via cheating."

"I do not cheat!"

"Of course, you don't. Fifty tickets for my pants, I think. Twenty for my shirt. Undergarments I have to think about." She put a coin in the machine and, after the balls descended, handed one to Atalant. "Better get rolling. There's an entrance fee, too."

All my clothes cost double then, Atalant shot back.

"Mmm. Deal." Without looking, Emn rolled a ball up the ramp and pocketed a corner slot. "Your turn. I'll give you twenty percent off the total tickets for *stuk*, too."

Atalant grabbed Emn by the waist and kissed her, forgoing any attempt at gentleness in the name of rebuttal.

She unbuttoned the top of Emn's jeans and sent, *I think this will even things even more.*

"You're competitive," Emn whispered, the words tickling the bottom of Atalant's lip.

"Don't you have some tickets to win? I'm competitive but I'm not cheap."

Emn giggled and spun away, making a show of inspecting every other available game while her pants slid lower and lower down her hips. "Focus on your strengths, Atalant. I'll meet you back at Skee-Ball in a moment."

"You're not allowed to pull those back up. Play where they land!"

The shrieking of an animatronic PLAYER ONE drowned out Emn's response. Atalant fed another coin into her machine and, when the wooden balls finished their descent, took a long breath and rolled the ball, underhand, into the dead center of the rings.

Four tickets came out. From behind her a machine yelled WINNER! FIFTY TICKETS!

"I just paid for your bra!" Emn cheered. "I, oh. That isn't going to help things. Are you sure I can't pull these up just a bit? The jeans are barely hanging onto my left hip."

"No." Atalant rolled another ball, this time hitting a corner circle. Twenty tickets came out. A quick wipe of *stuk* on her pants and she set another ball in the same place. Thickened with thoughts of Emn, the *stuk* gave her unexpected purchase on the porous wood.

"Shoot. This one just seems to take coins," Emn said from off to Atalant's left.

Atalant sunk balls four through eight into the fifty slot. Tickets spun from the machine like spaghetti, pooling next to her boot.

"Damn, this one just took my coin and didn't do anything," Emn said, jeans very nearly off her rear. "Maybe I'll come back to Skee-Ball."

"Shoo. This is my game." She smirked at Emn, slipped in another coin and decided that maybe, ball sports were her thing after all.

Glossary of Ardulan Talents

SCIENCE: Skills of creation including biology, chemistry, agriculture, design, art, healing, empathy, and telepathy.
Markings: three linked black circles on the inside of each wrist.

AGGRESSION: Skills of assertion, including innate knowledge of weapons, warfare, trade, land development, leadership, and exploration.
Markings: a variable number (usually seven to ten) of hexagons linked across the right side of the torso. Can span from armpit to hip.

HEARTH: skills of domesticity, including the arts of protection, shielding, child rearing, teaching, spiritual guidance, animal husbandry, public relations, and construction.
Markings: exactly four hexagons aligned side by side on the left shoulder.

MIND: skills of critical thinking, including piloting, problem assessment, mathematics, music, and physics.
Markings: a set of three equilateral triangles, intersecting at one point at the back of the left calf.

ELD: one who manifests a Talent at second *don* and another Talent at third *don*; a highly unusual occurrence.

FLARE: one who, upon their metamorphosis to Second Don, manifests *all* Ardulan Talents, including ones outside the normal Talent structure.

Noteworthy members of the Charted Systems

Spanning eighteen planets across six systems.

BALTEC - *Minoran System*

Minorans are the only known quadrupeds in the Charted Systems. There are seven species that all share the Minoran designation, and while genetically distinct, all can interbreed and produce viable offspring. All have melanin-based skin tones, as well as hair in several shades of brown. Hock spurs are present on two of the seven species; members of these species are seldom seen outside the Minoran System. Number of genders varies across species, however due to how closely related the species are, this is thought to be due to cultural mores rather than biology. Only one individual is required for reproduction, however fitness of the offspring increases with each genetically contributing parent.

EARTH - *Terran System*

Terrans are bipedal, with melanin-based skin. Hair color varies wildly across the species, as does the amount of body hair. Terrans have an unknown number of genders, as this statistic is consistently updated. Reproduction involves one from each of the dominant two genders (female and male), although trinary and even quaternary reproduction has been reported.

MISSOTONA - *Alusian System*

The Alusians are one species comprised of eleven subspecies, which are differentiated by the shape of scales sporadically interspersed across their carotenoid-based skin. Most are bipedal, and some of the subspecies are known to have fur. Alusians have two distinct genders (female and male), and variants thereof are so uncommon as to be statistically insignificant. Reproduction requires a parent from each gender.

NEEK - *Neek System*

The Neek are bipeds with similar stature and skin tone to Terrans. Unlike the Terrans, the Neek almost uniformly have red-hued hair, and none are capable of growing facial hair. Officially there is one species of Neek, however original Risalian survey data indicate the potential for either a second species, or a subspecies, that lacks melanin entirely. Dominant-species Neek have eight fingers per hand, with soft-keratin nails. They secret empathic mucous from their fingertips and, when under stress, from all of their sweat glands. The Neek have a trinary gender system (female, male, gatoi). Only two genders are required for reproduction, but the inclusion of a third gender increases fitness in the offspring.

OORIN - *Callis System*

The Oori are methane-based, phase-shifting organisms with a complicated biology. Little is understood about their physiology or reproduction. Outside of their native ecosystems, the Oori can be distinguished by the small cubes somewhere on their person that act as both an air filter and a translator, as their semi-viscous nature makes forming the sounds of Common difficult.

RISAL - *Risalian System*

The Risalians are a bipedal, agender species. While their skin tones are melanin-based, the unique density of their skin refracts light in such a way that the dark, high-molecular weight pigment appears as varying shades of blue. Most Risalians have dark hair and have an amphibious—instead of the more usual mammalian—evolutionary history. Breathing occurs through gill slits in the sides of the neck, although vestigial, mammalian-style noses are also present. Reproduction is accomplished through asexual budding. Of interesting note: Risalians are seldom seen without a secondary, companion species. While this species has no official name, they are also bipedal and appear to be reliant on the Risalians for care and direction.

Noteworthy members of the Alliance

Spanning twenty-seven planets across fifteen systems.

ARDULUM - *Yoshin System*

During its time in the Alliance, the Ardulan planet revolved around Yoshin as a large moon. The Ardulan people are bipeds with melanin-based skin, and are very similar to the Yishin and Keft in general appearance. They lack the heavier body hair of the Yishin and have a thinner keratin nail on their fingers (five per hand). Also Ardulan skin is quite thin, to the point of near translucence. While Ardulans have empathic mucous glands, no production of the mucous has ever been reported. Ardulans have three genders: female, male, and gatoi. All three are used for reproduction, although only two are necessary.

CRODEQUE - *Crodeque System*

The Quinns of Crodeque are not the dominant sentient species of their system, but are the only species willing to engage with the Alliance. All Quinns are gelatinous zooplankton, with a wide range of colors and forms. Most are fluid in their presentation and gender. There are forty-seven known genders within the Quinn, but only one Quinn is necessary for reproduction (though any number and combination is viable).

GGLLOT - *Ggyynii System*

The dominant sentient species of Ggllot are the Mmnnuggls. Bodies of Mmnnuggls are always perfectly spherical exoskeletons, with cartilaginous ears (usually two) appearing equidistant from one another. The casing of the exoskeleton has purple anthocyanin-based tones, and can range from true purple, to lilac, to near black, depending upon the mood of the Mmnnuggl. A given Mmnnuggl usually presents in one of four genders (primary female, primary male, secondary female, secondary male). Any combination of two genders is needed for reproduction, although all four may be used to no ill or additional positive effect.

KEFT - *Keft System*

The Keft people are bipedal, most with red-hued hair and melanin-based skin tones. Most have eight fingers per hand, the nails of which end in indigo or purple talons (ranging from 30-45mm long on average). Most Keft secret empathic mucous from their fingertips and, under stress, also from their sweat glands. A Keft usually presents in one of three genders (female, male, gatoi). Only two genders are required for reproduction, however the addition of the third genetic material increases fitness in the offspring.

XINAR - *Xinar System*

The Xinarn people, comprised of two genetically distinct but physically similar species, are bipeds with carotenoid-based skin tones and no body hair. Both species have between four to six fingers per hand. Each species has one gender, but reproduction takes one member from each species. Offspring belong genetically to one species or the other and are never blended.

YOSHIN - *Yoshin System*

The Yishin are bipeds very similar to the Keft, but differ in the length of their claws (generally less than 14mm long). Their bodies are covered in thick, orange hair that often obscures their melanin-based skin. Most Yishin secret empathic mucous from their fingertips and, under stress, also from their sweat glands. The Yishin have a trinary gender system (female, male, gatoi), with only two genders required for reproduction, but the addition of the third adding to the reproductive fitness of the offspring.

ACKNOWLEDGEMENTS

If you're holding this book and reading this, then thank you. This book would not exist without so many, many enthusiastic voices about Ardulum. From the shy fans who sneak up at conventions just to whisper how much they love the series and then skitter away, to the fans who post the beautiful fan art on Twitter, thank you. I've read your reviews, I've heard your stories, I've seen that glint in your eye when you ask about Yorden (because you didn't really think I'd kill him off, but then again, you don't know me that well yet, do you?).

The stories in this anthology serve two purposes. The first is to fill in the gaps in the (now rather extensive) Ardulum timeline. But the second is to give all the wonderful people who have asked for more a chance to see the stories that otherwise didn't really have a place in the original trilogy. Origin stories. Yorden as a central character, being a badass. Atalant and Emn just getting to kiss a lot. The secret life of gatois.

So, you don't have to say goodbye to Ardulum just yet. Take one final journey with me on the Pledge, on the Lucidity, on Ardulum itself, and let's give these characters the send-off they deserve. You've earned it. I've earned it. Atalant has definitely earned it.

Oh, and did I mention there are pictures?

ABOUT THE AUTHOR

J.S. Fields (@Galactoglucoman) is a scientist who has spent too much time around organic solvents. They enjoy roller derby, woodturning, making chain mail by hand, and cultivating fungi in the backs of minivans. You can find their books at www.jsfieldsbooks.com. To read more in the Ardulum universe, and more of J.S.'s work, join their Patreon at http://www.patreon.com/jsfields

Please take a moment to review this book at your favorite retailer's website, Goodreads, or simply tell your friends!